6.00

Until

the

Robin

Walks

on

Snow

Bernice L. Rocque

Until

the

Robin

Walks

on

Snow

3Houses

Trumbull, CT
www.3Houses.com

ISBN 978-0-9856822-1-7 (Paperback)

First Edition: September 2012
First Edition, revised: October 2012 (align with eBook)

This is dedicated
to those who came before us.

In seeing their essence—
we see ourselves.

Preface and Acknowledgements

I have been a family history researcher, on and off, for forty plus years. Back in the late 1960s, I had taken an interview note that one of my grandmother's children weighed one-and-a-half pounds at birth. When I was in my teens, I did not understand the significance of that statistic.

During a visit with my uncle and aunt (his wife) in late 2009, we talked about that birth and the question "how did they save such a tiny baby, born on the farm in 1922." I was about to decide what I would write next. (They were aware I had been writing memoir type material since 2004.) During our conversation, the "how did they do it" curiosity piqued for both my uncle and me. We agreed that it was a good mystery worth reconstructing, if we could.

We suspected that telling the story as nonfiction would be difficult, due to limited facts and the inability to ask the "characters" what happened. I recall suggesting that I could try to write the story as historical fiction, if my uncle would serve as an advisor. He was enthusiastic right from the start, so we began. Not long after that we drew his sister, my Aunt Vee, into the project. The goal was to start with facts, family history, and research—and then create the story that "might have happened."

My Uncle Tony and Aunt Vee have been a positive presence in my life from the time I was a small child. So many good memories I have! So, it is not a surprise to me that working on this story has been a joyful experience. Uncle Tony's wife, my Aunt Albina, was also fascinated from the moment the story took its first breath. Aunt Albina was my violin teacher extraordinaire, just the nicest combination of teacher and friend a young person could wish for. Despite advancing health issues, she has been a cheerful supporter in our challenge to tell this story. Her granddaughter, Anna, read her the final draft, chapter by chapter, and she loved it as if it were her own story.

In the course of two years, I contacted a number of my cousins and family friends to learn if anyone had more of this story's puzzle pieces. My cousin, Don, provided information that helped us understand what probably made the greatest difference in trying to save the baby. The Author's Notes following the story discuss this aspect further.

Bernice L. Rocque

Theresa Howard, a longtime friend of our family, began her life as a premature infant (weighing about three pounds) in the same time period. Her insights and comments were very useful, and her enthusiasm was energizing.

I so appreciate the time that family members have taken to review the initial and/or final draft of the manuscript. I'd like to thank Mike and Louisa, PJ, Monica, Anna, Donna, MaryLynn, Coni, Stevie and his family, distant cousin Barbara, and Evelyn, a cousin of my husband's, for the feedback they provided. Many of the comments changed the story's content or wording, and some of the feedback helped me to amplify the Author's Notes.

The review by friends widened my view on how prospective audiences outside the family might view the story. I would like to thank Steve Groth, Maureen Hayden, Dawn Larson, Carol Pisani, Susann Gill Riley, Mary Sanborn, Carl Serbell, and Tom Tumicki for their review of the story. A particular comment from one of these individuals helped me to correct an important error in the manuscript, and for that, I am particularly grateful. The feedback from friends helped me to refine the story, tune the dialogue, and understand how readers who were not family members might react to the various characters and situations. I also need to thank Mary Keane, who practically willed this book out of me, by regularly asking me how my book was coming. My intentions until this year were to produce a short story!

In the course of researching and verifying information, there were a number of organizations and people who helped me on multiple occasions.

I would like to thank the Office of the City Clerk in Norwich, Connecticut. Everyone there has been wonderful in answering the questions I had, and the records have been very easy to use there.

The reference staff of the Otis Public Library in Norwich deserves special note. Their local history room is a very comfortable environment in which to do research. Everyone I dealt with at Otis was professional, proactive, and cordial. Having once been a reference librarian who learned from the best—the best being my former colleague and long time friend, Celia Roberts, at the Simsbury Public Library, I have high standards! Celia, a librarian's librarian, has helped me numerous times over the years when I "hit a wall" in my genealogy research, and I want her to know how much I have appreciated her expert guidance.

Sometimes in research you come across someone who far exceeds your expectations. Such was my experience with Mary, the office manager at

Bernice L. Rocque

St. Joseph's Church in Norwich. She truly has the patience of a saint and deep knowledge of the church's records, its parishioners over time, and familiarity with Eastern European immigration to Norwich in the early 1900s. Our conversations and the records she located for me greatly assisted me in writing this and future stories.

Peter Shillo, one of the elders of St. Nicholas Russian Orthodox Church in Norwich, was very responsive in sharing obituaries of individuals I was researching. In addition, he provided a church anniversary brochure which had some valuable information on the founders of this church, including my relative Mikolaj Bychkowsky.

In my research of Helena, her husband, Mike, and Jan Sak, there were several individuals who dug deep into their family memories and records on my behalf to illuminate one or more of the story's characters. In sincere appreciation, I would like to acknowledge the help received from Jules Awdziewicz, Genevieve Erardy, Bill Falman, Peter Labenski, Joan Lenkiewicz, Matilda Matylewicz, and Jean Mockler.

Many works of fiction benefit by the review of experts. For this story, I relied on three groups of experts: medical, historical, and antique stove.

Erin Morelli, a current day midwife and descendent of friends of my grandparents, reviewed the manuscript and offered suggestions and questions which zeroed in on some of my underlying concerns about the pattern of development of extremely small premature infants.

Michael Morosky, MD, was able to resolve the issues Erin had raised, as well as review all medical aspects of the manuscript. Mike is a veteran OBY/GYN specialist, having delivered his 6,000[th] baby in 2012, an amazing achievement that made the local news, considering most obstetricians deliver about 2,500 babies in a career. Mike and I have known each other since the first grade, and he is still the nicest person, like a ray of light in the room. He so loves his work and I am grateful for the time he gave in reviewing this manuscript twice, as well as in reviewing the medical explanations in my Author's Notes. Mike also briefed me about why the infant might not have had some of the serious issues that extra small premature babies often have. Mike has been very encouraging about my writing and I am personally touched by his support.

When I was an undergraduate, Professor Bruce Stave at the University of Connecticut, made a lasting impression on me through his energetic and dramatic teaching. He made history as compelling as it really is. Because immigration at the turn of the twentieth century is one of his specialties, I asked if he would review the manuscript from a historical viewpoint, keep me safe, so to speak, which he did. He also provided some great suggestions that I was able to incorporate as part of the Author's Notes.

For their congenial help in increasing my understanding about how stoves in the 1920s worked, I am indebted to the father and son team, Emery and Brandon Pineo, who refurbish antique stoves in Rhode Island. Let's just say that I have a new appreciation for how skilled my grandmother must have been in managing her combination wood/coal stove. In the process, these stove experts conveyed how many stories they have heard about the important role that stoves (like the antique models they now rebuild) played in keeping babies warm and in helping premature infants to survive.

In 2004, when I made a decision to write stories about my family, I joined a writing group sponsored by the Trumbull Public Library. I have valued the fellowship as much as the knowledge that I have gained over the last seven years. The group reviewed two versions of the story and provided lots of ideas, a few hot debates, and so much encouragement. It has been a grand experience, especially during the years we were led by Charlie Slack. Members of the group have changed over time, but for their thoughts and insights about this story and the exciting realm of self-publishing, I would particularly like to thank Janet and Jim Bair, Barbara Benjamini, Bea Berger, Sharon Cohen, Bob Collins, Gloria Curry, John J. Gilmore, Carol Gursky, Rick Henrietta, Barbara MacMath, Mary Meli, Ann Pandya, Dori Rogers, Larry Russick, Maureen Stabile, and Jeannine Stauder.

For their professional contribution to this manuscript and its publication, I want to sincerely thank Jeff Lau, for the beautiful cover he designed, and Eileen Albrizio for her painstaking review and excellent editing suggestions.

My grandmother, my parents, and Aunt Nellie exited this world before this story became an idea, but their positive impact on my life is reflected in the threads of its chapters. I like to think they are close by, perhaps in another plane, and have heard me read aloud the words they inspired by being such talented, curious, and loving people during their lives. When they were here, they also answered every question I posed about family history. I wish I had asked them so many more!

Until

the

Robin

Walks

on

Snow

Prologue

The soft chimes of the Seth Thomas clock lifted Marianna from a shallow sleep. She opened her eyes but did not move. Her shoulders were wedged into the wood frame of the kitchen chair. Fearful of looking down, she turned her head toward the light.

By the east window, Helena was sitting up on the sofa, stretching her arms. The early morning rays of late November filtered through the tops of the trees at the edge of the woods. Marianna drifted for a moment, appreciating the stark, angular beauty of the scene.

"Good morning, Marianna. How is Antoni?"

The midwife's question jarred Marianna toward the eyes of her dearest friend. Such kind eyes—if only she could sink into their comfort. Marianna took a measured breath. It was time to check on her tiny son, resting on her chest, his skin to her skin. She looked into

Helena's eyes once again before inching the back of her hand toward the infant's shoulder.

His skin felt warm.

"He is alive, Helena. Antoni is alive." Marianna lightly grasped his arm and quietly sang his name, her eyes spilling the droplets of her relief.

Helena raised and clasped her hands in joy. After lighting the kerosene lantern, she picked up a small bowl from the short stack on the wood stove nearby and tiptoed over to Marianna.

"I hear his faint whimpering, Marianna. This is a good sign." The midwife handed the bowl to her friend.

"I was so worried. Helena—he is still alive!"

Helena touched her friend's shoulder. Then, she picked up the square pillow, placed it on Marianna's lap, and laid a small clean towel on top of it. Using both hands, Marianna moved the three-day-old to the towel. Helena looked the infant over and then wrapped the towel loosely around his fragile frame. Marianna massaged and squeezed her bulging

2

left breast until sticky milk oozed into the bowl. Immersing the blunt end of a small crochet hook, Marianna swirled it until the metal tip donned a light coating, just enough to brush on her baby's miniscule lips. She watched as the tip of Antoni's tongue appeared and disappeared, absorbing the first golden drop.

Helena whispered an *Our Father* and *Hail Mary*, and then rebuilt the fire in the wood stove. Marianna gazed at her friend. How relieved she was that Helena was handling the everyday chores. At twenty-five, Marianna thought herself a woman who could handle almost anything. She hated to admit that this birth had sapped her strength more than the four previous ones, if in a different way.

Marianna continued to rest her eyes on her friend. The midwife's face lit like sunshine, as if she was the mother of the newborn. With her porcelain skin, and blond hair twisted back in a graceful knot, Helena looked like an angel. Marianna knew what often happened to infants who were puny like this one. It was not uncommon for midwives and parents to conspire, put the weakling in a shoebox behind the stove and abandon it to the inevitable. Instead, Helena had kept up their spirits since the birth and made sure that the family was doing everything they could to keep this child alive.

Marianna felt the pressure of needing to use the chamber pot. Ignoring the discomfort for now, she fed her son as much of the thick milk as he would take. She thanked the Lord over and over on this bright Sunday morning for Helena's friendship and for the good fortune of the past few days.

Clockwise from Left:
Nikodimas, Marianna, Andrzej, Michal, Nellie.
Norwich, Connecticut, 1922.

Chapter One

When Marianna opened the door on the previous Thursday, Helena did not need to ask how her friend was feeling. The answer was written in the worry lines etched across Marianna's face, and in the dark straight hair that lay on her shoulders, unkempt, rather than twisted up neatly. They embraced and then sat many minutes before the midwife examined Marianna.

The baby was born later that afternoon, the twenty-third of November, 1922. The birth was relatively easy, but Marianna labored the last half hour in anguish, her mind picturing again and again the two babies that did not survive birth in the first years of her marriage to Andrzej. She forced her thoughts away from that sadness, remembering that, in 1918 and 1920, they were blessed with two healthy children, Nellie and Michal, now four and two.

Sweet tears streamed down Marianna's face when her new son took his first breath and then continued to breathe. While lightly cleaning off the baby, Helena reassured her friend that he appeared to be perfect, despite arriving more than two months early and weighing only a pound and a half according to the butter scale. Helena weighed him a second time to be certain.

The midwife wrapped the newborn in a small towel and placed him in the palm of his father's hand. Their son did not cry, and he did not move. Marianna watched as Andrzej stared at the infant's head. It was the size of a plum, but not that sickly bluish color of babies who lived but a few minutes. Andrzej slowly turned back the overlapping corners of the towel. His son's arms and legs were smaller around than his own little finger, with nails like specks. Ribs hardly big enough to hold a set of lungs protruded from the grayish chest. Its slight movement seemed an illusion.

Andrzej closed his eyes. He reached in his pocket for a handkerchief and wiped the beads of perspiration forming next to his wavy black

Bernice L. Rocque

hair. He did not look at his wife and she could see he was struggling to compose himself. Unable to stop the tears pooling in his eyes, he mouthed the words silently, "He is alive."

For Marianna, watching his despair brought to mind the story she had heard years before about her husband. Andrzej arrived in America in 1911 at age twenty-six, a few steps ahead of conscription into the Russian army. He went to live with his sister, Natalia, and her family. Andrzej adored his niece, Anna, born the year before he left Poland. While a toddler, Anna contracted whooping cough. Her condition worsened until one day, the doctor was called. He pronounced Anna dead. Andrzej refused to believe that this beloved child was gone. He had picked her up, rocked her in his arms, and tapped her back. To everyone's surprise, her eyes fluttered and then Anna began to cry. She eventually recovered from the illness.

Andrzej finally raised his eyes, their hazel color diluted in his watery gaze. He and his wife did not always get along, but Marianna nodded just enough for him to see they were one at this moment. He turned towards the midwife.

"Helena, can you help us?" Andrzej's eyes blinked rapidly, but his voice was becoming firmer. "We must save our son. We must."

"I will do everything I can," Helena promised. She took a deep breath and then leaned toward Andrzej. "If it is God's will, we will save your newest son." She lifted the infant gently from his father's hand and whispered, "We must keep the baby warm." Helena placed the newborn inside Marianna's blouse, his little chest to his mother's chest. Then, she draped a light blanket around mother and child. "He will hear his mother's heartbeat. I will cut some small diapers. We have done what we can until Marianna's milk comes."

Helena shooed the men from the room and washed the fluids and perspiration from her friend's weary body. "Marianna, I will fix your hair tomorrow morning."

Marianna forced a small smile before turning to look again at the child, a lump of flesh so frail in appearance that she was fearful of touching him.

Bernice L. Rocque

* * *

The midwife removed the wet and bloodied birth linens and set them to soak outside in two large wash tubs filled earlier with cold well water. Helena watched from the well pump as Marianna's father, Nikodimas, carried the afterbirth and cord out to the edge of the field near the woods. While she tended the linens, he dug a deep hole and buried the bundle. After wiping his face and neck with his sleeve, Nikodimas rested on his shovel handle and looked toward the western sky.

Helena decided to walk to where he was. The midwife hoped she was not intruding on a moment he preferred to spend in privacy. She stood by his side, relaxing in the late afternoon glow of the setting sun.

"Perhaps the lingering light on this mild November day was meant to give us hope, Nikodimas."

"Ah, Helena. The days ahead will be difficult, while we try to keep the child alive." Nikodimas removed his spectacles and wiped them using the front of his shirt.

"Nikodimas, love surrounds this child, even if he appears more vulnerable than any newborn we have ever seen. We will work together. Maybe the Lord will grant us a miracle."

"Perhaps. My Paulina and I lost all six of Marianna's brothers when they were infants or children. I know the fear that is squeezing my daughter's heart."

"Yes, I know you do, Nikodimas. In the next few days... Well, I do not wish to worry you, but even birth mothers without sadness can drift into darkness. We must be vigilant, and keep her mind busy."

"Yes, you are right, Helena."

"Before the night comes, perhaps a short walk would do us both some good, Nikodimas. I need to inform my husband that I will be away a few days."

"Then, I am happy to escort you to the home of the veterinarian. He is a generous man. We have used his telephone on a few other occasions."

"I will get my coat, Nikodimas, and tell Marianna where we are going."

Bernice L. Rocque

Just as the long dusk was ending, Nikodimas and Helena returned from the walk. As she entered the kitchen, the first thing Helena saw was Marianna sitting very still in the kitchen chair. The midwife's friend was staring out the window, but not looking at anything. Helena could hear the soft sounds of the newborn trying to get his mother's attention, but Marianna seemed unaware.

Helena thought back to how, during the birth, Marianna had acted distraught from the moment she realized her baby was coming far too early. Marianna's sinking mood was difficult to manage then, and it would not be useful now.

Helena knelt by her friend. She thought a soft, firm voice would be best.

"Marianna?" Helena waited for her friend's eyes to blink. "Marianna, we will talk now about tomorrow. Your son will need to be fed often, every hour during the day and every two in the night."

Marianna said nothing at first. Then, she turned her head towards her friend. "Helena, how will I feed him the thick milk when it comes?" The fret poured from Marianna's throat, like milk from a pitcher. "I cannot use my finger. It will hurt him, no?"

Helena cradled her friend's hands. "Marianna, you are right to be concerned."

"And, if I give him too much at once, Helena, he might choke." The midwife stood and grabbed the handle of the lantern that Nikodimas had lit before he went upstairs. The baby had fallen asleep and looked peaceful with his cheek to Marianna's chest. Helena leaned to the side so that she could just see the infant's mouth. It was barely visible, a grayish blue line on the little face.

"Marianna, let me look around."

While drawers in the kitchen flew open and shut, the contents rattling now and then from Helena's quick searching, Marianna offered suggestions. The midwife complimented her friend on the ideas as she continued to hunt for a tool that would give Marianna more control.

Bernice L. Rocque

In the sitting room, Helena scanned the shelves of the dark oak hutch.

"Marianna, I see something." To the right of the mirror, on a shelf away from the reach of the children, was a small metal crochet hook. Helena picked it up and presented it to her friend.

Marianna's pale blue eyes sharpened for the first time that day.

"Yes, Helena! Yes, the blunt side might work. Good, we will try it tomorrow when my milk comes." Marianna's changed expression pleased the midwife.

"I will bathe it in boiling water first," Helena announced. Ladling some water into the tea kettle, the midwife added, "Nothing but the cleanest implements for our precious child!" She smiled at Marianna and then to herself.

The farmhouse and immediate surroundings.
Norwich, Connecticut.
Sketch by A.C.J.

Chapter Two

The household quieted for the night later than usual, the delivery having delayed their supper. In the kitchen, Marianna was dozing, the stuffing around her in the chair supporting mother and child. Helena reclined on the kitchen sofa, so overtired she remained wide awake. *The infant is not struggling to breathe. Why is this?*

Helena had witnessed the exhaustion of numerous small babies, watching them gasp for air for minutes or hours, or sometimes days before they expired. Marianna's first child had struggled to breathe for thirty minutes before returning to the Lord. If this newborn survived, it would be weeks before he was out of danger. *If we can get him to feed. If he can digest the milk. If we can preserve Marianna's strength.* Helena felt her body shaking. *I must have faith. I must. The Lord will decide.* She closed her eyes and tried to quiet her mind, but it was no use. She kept thinking about Marianna.

Helena knew her friend might try to do too much, too soon after the birth. Marianna had accomplished a mountain of work in the past few months. *Perhaps this is why she delivered early and why the baby is so small?* That no longer mattered... She would not open her heart about this to Marianna, heaping guilt on the load of worry.

Helena thought she might have done the same. She had seen the property when her friends were considering it. The two-story house, with the row of hundred-foot Norway spruce out front, pretty shutters, and wrap-around porch was far better looking outside than inside. The property came with a barn, a few sheds that would be useful, apple trees, and thirteen acres of land.

In the middle of the summer, relatives of Andrzej had alerted him about the farmhouse and land, near the top of Bean Hill in Norwichtown. Andrzej told Helena he liked the location, only one mile from the streetcar, and not too far from three mills where he might get

Bernice L. Rocque

work. With two children and another expected, it was time to move from their cramped apartment downtown.

Helena remembered when Nikodimas got his first glimpse of the land. He had placed his hand over his heart. Marianna's father pointed out the privacy the property offered and the farm's potential, with its gently sloping woods and flat pastures on one of the highest points in Norwich. "The house is a minor problem." Nikodimas had remarked. "It is not the best constructed. But, it is not the worst." It was simple to him! "Some scrubbing, carpentry, and paint will make it into a fine home for my daughter and her family." Marianna's father had asked around. He was certain the price could be negotiated.

When Marianna stood back from the house, she saw its condition, but trusted her father's opinion that they could make it livable. Helena remembered Marianna's surprise at finding no flower gardens. *Yes, splashes of color would make this Marianna's home.* Helena's friend had talked for years about planting iris, poppies, pinks, and all kinds of herbs to flavor her cooking and heal her family when they were ailing. In anticipation that they might move to the farm, Marianna had asked some friends on High Street for a root section of an iris she had admired.

Marianna had confided to Helena that, despite six years of savings, the couple did not have enough cash to purchase the property. Helena had worried that Andrzej would be too proud to accept money from Marianna's father. After days of thinking about the situation and gentle persuasion from all sides, Andrzej signed a $1,000 promissory note to his father-in-law, letting his wife know hours later that knots still tied his stomach. Nikodimas had said he understood Andrzej's hesitation, so he assured his son-in-law that the loan would be forgiven if either of the two men perished. The well intended words had some value to Andrzej, but all could see he had the feeling of an anvil hanging from his neck, and as Marianna told Helena, it was especially heavy before he fell asleep each night.

Helena had observed the shudder in Andrzej's body when he explained to her that,

Bernice L. Rocque

with the loan's interest rate at six percent, the obligation to Nikodimas would probably take more than ten years to repay. It came due twice each year, at the same time as the taxes. Helena figured that Andrzej would need to be working more steadily. She could picture Andrzej rolling his eyes as he imagined how many expenses there would be in the first few years on this farm. And of course, he could not forget his young children. They would outgrow things quickly. Marianna could not sew everything the children needed.

It was Nikodimas who lightened the mood about the obligation. A few days after the contract was signed and the property was theirs, Marianna's father suggested that the family celebrate by sitting for a portrait at the Antoofian studio on Main Street. Nikodimas remarked afterwards that his wife, Paulina, in Lithuania, would be very happy to see how prosperous and healthy the family looked. He mailed her one of the photographs on the day before they moved from 27 High Street to the Bean Hill farm.

Helena laughed to herself, first thinking of the photograph and how impressive they all appeared in their Sunday best clothes, and then recalling how Marianna had refused to move into the roach infested Civil War-era farmhouse until it was fumigated and thoroughly cleaned. She and Marianna scrubbed the floors for hours, their knees blistering and their hands becoming red and raw from the lye soap. The late September weather was warm enough to sleep out in the barn for several nights. Their bodies had dropped into the soft hay and instant sleep not long after the dusk.

Each time Helena visited for a few days, Marianna spoke of the urgency to make the most of every gift from neighbors and friends, as well as the bartered goods that Andrzej and Nikodimas collected by helping others with the fall harvest and slaughtering on nearby farms. On three occasions, Nikodimas, Andrzej, and Marianna spent the day together out in the gray shed—carving, salting, and smoking meat for the winter months, while Helena watched the children.

Bernice L. Rocque

Deer and rabbit were plentiful on the land her friends had purchased. When Nikodimas killed a young buck a few days before Marianna gave birth, Andrzej and Marianna wasted no time in returning some of their obligation for the gifts they had received. They shared part of the meat and organs with their generous neighbors. When Helena and Nikodimas had walked down the street to the veterinarian's house after the birth, he had roared in laughter as he told her the story, saying how much of the deer disappeared before his eyes. He joked that their family was like a flock of robins descending on the tasty worms in the same patch of grass.

The days did not seem long enough to Marianna. The sun was setting earlier each week. Marianna had canned bushels of the fall fruits, sewed curtains, stuffed pillows, and stitched additional quilts using the goose down and the ticking fabric brought by friends. In the old country, Marianna learned to sew in the domestic school that Lithuanian girls attended, while her brothers attended school in Germany a short distance across the Nemunas

River. Helena put her hand over her mouth as she caught herself laughing out loud. Her friend so detested sewing! Though a skilled seamstress, Marianna preferred crocheting, and had dressed the furniture with cotton lace doilies and bureau scarves "knotted" since coming to America.

Busy from dawn until dark on the farm, and though exhausted at the end of each day, Marianna had felt fine. When the October sun warmed the air and colored leaves floated down around them, she and Marianna had picked mushrooms in the woods, or taken afternoon walks with Nellie and Michal to forage for nuts. Sometimes Andrzej or Nikodimas would join them and the expedition would become a giant game to see who could pick up the most nuts. The empty flour sacks filled quickly, and in the process the family located numerous hickory and shagbark trees, as well as clusters of hazelnut bushes that they marked in their minds.

Helena fondly remembered one of their earliest trips. Nikodimas had continued the game after they returned home. How he

Bernice L. Rocque

tromped around and carried on with those children! That day, Nellie hunted for a "nice flat rock, not too heavy," that her grandfather wanted for a base, and a rounded stone that would mold to his hand to use as a cracker. When she found them, Nikodimas sat down, straddling the lowest step of the porch stairs. He cracked the nuts, hitting just hard enough to fracture the shell but not smash it. When he offered the nutmeat to the children, he whispered his "secret" to Nellie and Michal. "The shagbarks are my favorite. See how their thin shell protects such delicious treasure."

The children giggled and put out their hands.

"Ah, you want more nuts," their grandfather had cried. He hugged and tickled one, and then the other, until they were squealing with laughter. He teased them, as their father and mother often did, saying they were "little swinias." Nellie and Michal loved being called little piglets. It was an excuse to wrap their arms around their grandfather's neck and sing the songs he had taught them. Nikodimas raucously joined in with his melodious voice and the air filled with their happiness.

Helena felt warm inside as she thought about that golden afternoon. But, her friend had viewed it differently. Marianna had watched her children collect and gobble up the nuts that day, and although a smile spread across her face, her eyes were glassy and turned downward at moments. When Helena asked if something was wrong, Marianna dug into her skirt pocket and showed Helena the letter she had received that week from Lithuania. Marianna said she regretted that her mother was missing these moments with Nellie and Michal. Helena could hear the sadness in her voice as Marianna exclaimed in frustration, "If only I could send these moments to my mother in a neatly tied up package!" They had dreamed about a possible trip back to Lithuania to visit, but Marianna was unsure if it would ever happen. Helena had reminded Marianna that she needed to be thankful. Her father was with them for now.

Nellie and Michal might have watched the deft demonstrations of their grandfather for

Bernice L. Rocque

hours. But, when Marianna signaled her father that the children had eaten enough, Nikodimas carried the remaining nuts to the root cellar. He emptied them into a barrel, covered them over with a few old pieces of board, and placed the cracking stones on top. Helena smiled, remembering how she could not resist following the children down the steps into the cellar, where Nikodimas explained that the stones would keep the clever mice from getting into their stash.

Like Marianna, the men worked from the first light each day, except when Andrzej could find work as a laborer or when Nikodimas needed to attend to his business. They cut and brought in hay, split wood, and before turning over the soil, salvaged the remnants of a few paltry crops left behind by the previous owner. There were still many repairs to make before winter white covered the land.

On weekends, their friend, Jan Sak, would drive from downtown Norwich to help Andrzej and Nikodimas. Helena reflected that they all laughed a lot when Jan was around. He would tell them silly stories and jokes that he heard from friends and shopkeepers. Jan could strike up a conversation with anyone, about anything, and bring smiles. Marianna, her father, and Andrzej welcomed his company whenever he wanted to stop by. Jan in turn seemed pleased to spend time with them, helping with some of the farm chores and enjoying the home-cooked meals and whiskey—when they had some.

Helena felt fortunate about the friends she had in America. Before she fell asleep on the night of the birth, Helena prayed for a miracle, prayed that all the important things would happen right. Most mothers were back to responsibilities within ten days of giving birth, and even by then the fathers were complaining about loss of sleep. Marianna would need to devote all her attention, hour after hour, for weeks or perhaps months, to this tiny infant. Before she fell asleep, worry sat like a boulder in Helena's heart.

Bernice L. Rocque

Chapter Three

On the morning after the birth, Helena went outside to the privy, like usual, but instead of heading straight back to the house afterwards, she went to the barn to speak to the men. They must have viewed the serious expression on her face, because both Andrzej and Nikodimas immediately halted their chores.

Helena stood very still for a moment, her eyes closed. Then she spoke. "I have never birthed a baby this small, nor heard of one." The midwife took a deep breath, and then looked down at the ground and around the barn. Tears welled up in her eyes. "Marianna will be heartbroken if this child does not survive."

"Yes, Helena. I know." Nikodimas took a deep breath, and then looked over at his son-in-law.

Andrzej tipped his head slightly and then reflected out loud. "This is the second son she named Antoni, after her favorite brother. Helena, did you know that Marianna's brother, Antanas, drowned while swimming in the Nemanus River?"

Helena nodded slowly and made the sign of the cross.

"I do not know how..." Andrzej mumbled, "how you bore the loss of so many sons, Nikodimas—before they reached manhood."

"Each time, it felt like the blood left my body. As for Paulina, her pain was far greater than mine, I think. Many years have passed since that sadness, but I must believe that everything happens for a purpose. I might never have brought Marianna to America if my sons had lived."

"I am so glad Marianna came. I love my friend." The midwife looked away from the men. She had not expected to spill her heart this way. When her eyes finally met theirs, she realized they were waiting patiently for her to continue. Helena spoke the words slowly. "Marianna must give her attention to the

Bernice L. Rocque

baby—only to the baby. I have talked with her about this and her head moves up and down."

Helena raised her eyebrows.

Nikodimas extended one arm toward Helena and the other toward Andrzej, chuckling before he said, "But, we all know Marianna well!"

A cascade of laughter by the three broke the tension.

"My friend packs more work into a day than even three of the most productive people!" Helena shook her head. "How will she just sit?"

Andrzej reached over and grasped the midwife's hands. "Thank you, Helena, for everything you have done. I understand the situation is serious."

"You are most welcome, Andrzej." Looking back and forth at both of them, she added, "Of course, as Marianna's friend, I will do everything I can do to make things easier."

Nikodimas leaned toward Helena, the palms of his hands extended, and his voice low and steady. "But as Marianna's midwife, you have thoughts about how we must proceed, yes?"

"It is important that I be honest with you both." Helena stared directly into Andrzej's eyes for a second, and then at Nikodimas. "If this newborn continues to survive, it will be two months or more, before Marianna can return to her duties. She must keep the child close to the warmth of her body."

Andrzej sighed. "If there is anything else I can do, please ask me. Marianna is very independent, yes? Sometimes it is not obvious to me that help is needed."

"I have concern—about distractions. They could affect Marianna's milk." Helena clutched her hands and arms to her chest. "Even though she will be tired, she may become frustrated and get up to do things if she feels they are left undone too long. We must avoid this." Helena shifted her weight and gave them time to react.

Nikodimas stroked his moustache with his fingertips. "Helena, what are your thoughts on how we can remove this temptation from Marianna's view?"

Helena grinned at Nikodimas. "Oh, how I wish I could describe things as you do!"

Before Nikodimas could respond, Andrzej spoke. "Then you have some particular suggestions, Helena?"

"Yes, Andrzej. It would be good if we divide her usual chores. I can tend to Marianna, do the cooking, cleaning, washing, and look after the children when both of you are occupied."

"And, if we collect the eggs, churn the butter, make the cheese, and the like, then Marianna will not have a reason to turn her attention, even for a minute."

"Andrzej, this is exactly what I have been thinking."

"We all want to save my son. Please do not worry any further, Helena." Glancing over at his father-in-law, Andrzej stated, "Nikodimas and I will discuss this and agree on responsibilities."

They did not react the way she had expected, like other men she knew. Helena realized they must have had conversations, just like she and Marianna.

"There is one other thing that I would like to ask," Helena said.

"Of course. What is it?" Andrzej replied.

"The chimes of the clock in the sitting room are beautiful, but I can tell that Marianna is not accustomed to sleeping so near the sound. For some reason she changes the subject when I bring it up."

"Helena, the clock was a gift from Nikodimas," Andrzej explained. "I know she treasures it." He slowly turned towards his father-in-law.

"It will be easiest if I handle this," Nikodimas offered. "I will move it to the parlor when we return to the house. And, Helena, can I depend that you will tell me if we need to banish the clock further?"

"Yes, of course! Thank you, Nikodimas."

Helena told them that she would go home to High Street in the next week and also register the baby's birth downtown. At thirty-one, Helena had delivered scores of children, learning from an experienced midwife in the old country when she was a girl. Nikodimas and Andrzej walked with Helena out of the barn. She could feel their eyes follow her up the slight incline to the house.

Chapter Four

After getting the wood stove going on the first Sunday morning of Antoni's life, Helena emptied the chamber pot that Marianna had used, washed her hands, and then started the breakfast. She cooked up oatmeal for everyone, brewed some chicory coffee, and fetched two apples from the root cellar to cut up in the oatmeal.

Despite their worries, Marianna's thick milk had come the day after the birth. Another day had passed, though, before Antoni showed any interest, creating anxiety in the household and much debate about what to do. Concerned about dehydration, his father had suspended a wet spoon every hour above the baby's mouth, releasing a few water droplets. Finally, late on Saturday, the baby consumed the first drops of his mother's golden thick milk.

Every muscle in Marianna's body had been tight for three days and nights. She would not permit her body to doze more than an hour or two. She counted the chimes in her half sleep and when she opened her eyes, her heart pounded as she reached to touch her son's shoulder. Each time that Antoni felt warm, her body released all its tension, as if melting like gelatin. Marianna admitted to Helena that she had wept more in the past few days than at any time in her life. She could not control the tears of joy.

As the sun rose on his first Sabbath, Antoni took in a good amount of the golden nourishment that his mother dabbed on his lips using the handle end of her crochet hook. Afterwards, she and Helena ate some breakfast, and since there was still no movement by the family upstairs, Helena held Antoni while Marianna washed. Before she put on a clean blouse, Marianna began to collect some milk for the next feeding.

"Helena, see how my milk is changing."

Marianna squeezed her right breast again. A steady stream of white milk filled the small bowl.

"This is very good, Marianna." The midwife walked the few steps into the sitting room, reached down behind the rocking chair, and then returned to the kitchen. Marianna wondered what Helena was searching for in her medical case. A broad smile suddenly appeared on the midwife's face. She drew out a small glass jar containing an eyedropper and held it in front of Marianna.

"Come to the light." Helena said, stepping to the window and parting the half curtain.

Once her friend was sitting comfortably on the kitchen sofa with the newborn in front of her on a pillow, Helena filled the eyedropper and demonstrated how to wake the infant gently and then dribble just a little of the opaque milk onto his lips. Antoni's tongue took in the thinner milk more quickly than Marianna expected, as if the newborn knew the delicious liquid was waiting just for him, behind the golden early milk. Antoni consumed a few drops before the rest of the family began to stir upstairs.

Marianna loved the sounds of the household wakening, the feathery footsteps of her children, and the heavier, slower ones of her husband and her father. Nellie came first, running down the staircase and prancing through the narrow front hall and sitting room. Stopping short at the entrance to the kitchen and scuffing her shoes lightly, the little girl walked to the sofa and stood next to her mother in the warm sunshine streaming through the east window.

"Matka, can I touch him?"

Marianna drew the child close and planted a kiss on each cheek. "My dear Nellie, see how our Antoni is having his breakfast now. Just whisper a good morning to him."

The little girl looked up at her mother and Helena before turning towards her baby brother. She whispered, "Good morning, little brother."

Nellie watched as her mother released a pearl of milk from the eyedropper. Her brother's bottom lip began to quiver, and then moved slowly back and forth, smearing the white drop just a little. Then, his tiny tongue glided in and out, like a miniature machine, until the drop thinned and his lips glistened.

Bernice L. Rocque

"Antoni's mouth is so little, Matka."

"Yes, my Nellie. That is why we are using the eyedropper. See how your brother likes the milk!"

"Like a bee to honey," Helena crooned while spooning out a small dish of oatmeal and pouring in some cream.

As Helena situated Nellie at the table in the sitting room, Nikodimas appeared with two-year-old Michal, and a few minutes later Andrzej joined them. The doting grandfather propped up Michal by placing a pillow on his seat. After Helena set the rest of the bowls on the table, Andrzej bowed his head.

"Dear Lord, we give our thanks for this nourishing breakfast and for protecting our family, especially our newest son. Amen."

Within a few minutes the oatmeal had vanished from all the bowls on the sitting room table. Helena poured coffee for Andrzej and Nikodimas, and then coffee milk for the children, which she made earlier by infusing a pitcher of rich milk with just a little hot coffee.

"It is a fine morning for a story," Nikodimas suggested, after stirring in some cream and taking a sip of coffee. Is anyone interested in hearing the story about the three brothers?"

"Yes, Dziadzia," the children replied, clapping their hands. Everyone seemed enthusiastic about hearing the story, except for Andrzej. The boredom showed in his face, as Marianna and Helena pulled their kitchen chairs nearer the entryway to the sitting room. Andrzej had heard the tale and told the tale, too many times. His father-in-law tended to weave the tale about Lech, Cech, and Rus a bit differently each time, even working Lithuania into the story on occasion, even though the legend had never included Lithuania. Andrzej was looking at the happy expressions on his children's faces when Nikodimas began.

"There was once a wise king who had many children and grandchildren. The kingdom had prospered so much during his long reign that by the time he died there were far too many people living there. The land could no longer produce enough food for everyone. Even wild game was becoming scarce! This was concerning because there were many grandchildren of marrying age who would soon start their own families. So, the king's three youngest sons, Lech, Cech, and Rus, and their families, decided to leave the kingdom and find new homes."

"Were they sad to leave?" Nellie asked.

"Of course they were. But, their situation was serious," Nikodimas emphasized. "They trusted that God would help them. Their faith made it easier to see the journey as an adventure."

"Story?" Michal requested shyly.

"Ah, yes. I have only just begun. The three families walked toward the south for days and days, crossing fields and rivers until there were no houses and no people in sight. At sunset one night, the families reached a forest of gigantic trees."

"How big were the trees, Dziadzia?" Nellie asked.

"Oh, they were as tall as the trees in front of our house."

Nellie slid out of her seat and ran to the window to look out at the row of Norway spruce. When she sat down again, she nodded to her grandfather and closed her eyes. "I can see the tall trees now."

"Then I will continue. Since it was already getting dark in this forest of tall trees, the families rolled out their blankets and went to sleep. The next morning, the three brothers climbed one of the tallest trees on the edge of the forest to see what they could see. As they climbed higher and higher up the tree, the view of the surrounding lands got better and better. The children and grandchildren of the three brothers stood below, waiting patiently to hear. Finally, Cech yelled down, 'there are low mountains to the south.' Then, Rus shouted, 'there are rivers and lakes in the flatlands to the east,' his deep voice projecting clearly to his clan."

Nikodimas looked into Michal's eyes and then Nellie's. He mouthed the next word slowly. "Suddenly—"

"The white eagle flew into the nest!" Nellie giggled. "I remember the story, Dziadzia."

"Yes, you did. This majestic white eagle flew above their heads, landing on the edge of her nest."

Michal laughed. "Big white bird."

"Yes, Michal. Lech was quite impressed with this pure white bird. He told his brothers that the eagle was a sign from heaven. But, Cech and Rus were not paying attention to Lech. The two were already climbing down the tree, discussing the direction their families would go."

"They were afraid of the bird, I think."

"You might be right, Nellie."

"Were baby birds in the nest, Dziadzia?"

"I wonder!" Nikodimas replied, with a wink to Nellie and then to Michal.

"Lech let the eagle be and followed his brothers down the tree, where soon, he saw his two brothers conversing with their families. After much talk, Cech and his tribe decided to head south to the rolling hills and low mountains. His kingdom became the country of Czechoslovakia. Rus and his tribe traveled east toward the lakes and rivers. His kingdom became Russia."

"Dziadzia, I remember the next part of the story."

"You do?"

"Lech stayed in the land of the eagle," Nellie responded.

"He did. He started a kingdom near the tree where he first saw the white eagle. The new kingdom was called Poland. Lech and his tribe were happy for many years in their new homeland. The family grew vegetables and grains, raised animals, hunted the game of the forest, and the men fought in wars when it was necessary. Sometimes they won the wars and remained free, and sometimes they lost and were ruled by other tribes. Many generations of children were born. They grew into men and women, and eventually died, as happens in life. A thousand years passed. And now..."

Nikodimas raised his eyebrow and took a sip of coffee.

"There were too many people—again!" Nellie gushed. She and Michal began to giggle and everyone else began laughing as well.

"That is right. There was not enough food and not enough work. The rulers forbade the people from practicing their religion and receiving education in their own language. Furthermore, the despicable rulers did not

Bernice L. Rocque

hesitate to force many of the young men into their armies. So, what did the people do, Nellie—just sit and feel sorry for themselves?"

"No, Dziadzia. They came to America!" Nellie announced with a giant smile, to nods and chuckles in the sitting room and the entryway to the kitchen.

"Well! That is the story of the three brothers. Now there are a few chores to do."

"Can we help, Dziadzia?"

"But of course."

"That will be acceptable," Andrzej stated. "We will not go to Mass today. Your Matka and Antoni may need our help."

Nikodimas held onto Michal while the toddler slid down from his chair. The children loved to feed the chickens and help milk the cow, especially when they each got a nice squirt or two of milk. Their grandfather always let them try their hand and answered their questions with patience and love. On their way back from the barn, Nikodimas carried an armful of wood to the side porch. Then, because it was the day of the Lord, they all rested.

Chapter Five

On the following Thursday, Andrzej's relatives from Fitchville stopped by early in the morning for a short visit. Nellie was excited because their daughter, Sally, was with them.

Mikolaj Bychkowsky greeted Andrzej in Russian and handed him a grain sack. Andrzej took the bag with both hands.

"Ah, wonderful!" Andrzej declared after moving closer to the lantern and peeking into the weighted sack. "Marianna, they have brought us two freshly killed chickens."

"My boss at work reminded me that here in America, they call this day Thanksgiving and often serve poultry," Mikolaj said.

Andrzej thanked the Bychkowskys for their generous gift, and then leaned towards his wife, Marianna, who was sitting in the kitchen chair with her arm supporting the body of their new son. Marianna bowed her head slightly in appreciation of the gift and

Bernice L. Rocque

lifted Antoni so the visitors could see him. As the Bychkowskys stood back looking somewhat dazed, Helena offered everyone some coffee milk which Marianna liked to leave warming in an enamel pot on the stove for whenever they wanted it. They declined politely, trying to mask their shock after viewing what Marianna knew looked like a stick of flesh resting on her chest. While whispering their goodbyes, the wife, Savetta, asked if Marianna had occupied the kitchen chair since Antoni was born.

Marianna grimaced. She did not know Savetta well, but in the tone of her voice she heard concern in the Russian words.

"Ah, yes—many hours!"

"It is good that the back of the wood chair reclines."

"Yes, I can nap when my son naps without worrying that I will fall forward."

"It is difficult to sit a long while."

"Oh yes. Many aches I have—in my back, my arms, my legs. It is to be expected. When I feel stiff, I get up and walk around or I move to the kitchen sofa and rest there for a little while." Marianna laughed nervously, the dangling strand of rosary beads in her hand shaking for a moment.

"Close to Marianna's warmth is the best place for the baby," Helena said, "until he is out of danger."

Helena spoke the Russian words with a gentle authority. Marianna wondered what her husband's relatives were thinking. *If he lived, how long would it be before he was out of danger?* She feared they might think her foolish, trying to save this handful of skin and bones, or perhaps they thought her lazy, that she would rather sit than tend to her duties. Marianna felt the heat of their eyes on her. Eyes that held what, pity perhaps? She waited for a pause in the conversation and then spoke, her words tumbling out faster than she intended.

"I am thankful. Our son is a gift from heaven. He is breathing quietly and does not seem to be in distress. Helena has guided us well." Marianna closed her eyes for a moment and quickly made the sign of the cross.

"It is fortunate that Marianna is in good health and able to keep Antoni close to her." Nikodimas added. "We are all trying to help, but our efforts are modest compared to what Marianna is doing. I am concerned that she is not getting good sleep, but for now that cannot be helped."

"God willing, when Antoni gets stronger, the wood stove will keep him warm instead of my body." Marianna coughed, from speaking too rapidly.

While pouring a glass of water for Marianna, Helena added, "Today, Antoni is a week old. We are all giving love every minute to this precious child, but still praying to the Blessed Mother."

"And to Saint Michal," Andrzej whispered. Leaning toward his relatives, he added, "Do you recall that our eldest son was born on the feast of the powerful Archangel?" Andrzej raised his eyes and arms to the heavens. "So, we humbly appeal to Saint Michal, hoping he has an interest in our family and in protecting our Michal's new brother."

On hearing his name, Michal had grabbed the trousers of his grandfather and snuggled into them. Nellie, standing by Marianna's side, leaned into her mother's shoulder with a quizzical look on her face. The children did not hear Russian words often enough to remember their meaning.

However, there were immediate gestures of understanding from the adults, especially from Mikolaj Bychkowsky, who at six feet tall was almost a head taller than Nikodimas and Andrzej. Dropping to one knee near little Michal, Mikolaj patted the toddler's shoulder and then sat down on the floor next to him. The two-year-old winced and looked up at his grandfather.

"We can appreciate what you are saying, Andrzej." Nikodimas mused. Many believe that our fate is written before we are born, but that the holy family and the saints do intervene, on occasion. It does not hurt to humbly request assistance and also take the actions we believe will save a life, as long as we understand that the outcome is not ours to decide."

Bernice L. Rocque

As if he was suddenly invigorated, Mikolaj Bychkowsky appeared to forget his inclination to keep the visit short. He leaned back on his elbows, stretching his lanky frame on the floor next to little Michal who moved even closer to his grandfather.

"Mikolaj," Nikodimas whispered. "I do not think little Michal remembers you from your last visit."

"True. And I must look very big to him!"

"As Michal grows he will learn what we all know. Yes, Mikolaj Bychkowsky is a big man— with a big mind."

"You are very kind, Nikodimas." Mikolaj stroked his moustache, his hand covering part of the flush in his face. "I confess," he laughed, "I have another question on my mind."

"We expect no less, Mikolaj!" Andrzej complimented. "Please share your question."

"It is about the stove." The deep voice hesitated. "How will you keep this unusually small baby just the right temperature—warm enough, but not too warm?"

"I can hear the concern in your question, Mikolaj. This is exactly why Helena and I will make tests," Marianna stated.

"I think you are doing the right thing. Do you know yet where you will place the baby overnight?" Mikolaj asked.

This question led into a long discussion and friendly debates about the merits of positioning an infant behind, to the side, or in front of the stove. All shared stories about small infants from their experiences, here in America and in the old country. Marianna listened carefully. There might be something new that she and Helena could consider. She and her father had discussed many of the same subjects.

"My daughter, Marianna, has a talent for working the stove," Nikodimas said. Extending his bent arm toward the company he added, "She learned this from her mother in Lithuania, a wonderful baker of all kinds of breads." He closed his eyes, leaned his head back, and breathed in deeply as if enjoying the scent of a faraway loaf.

Marianna chuckled along with everyone else at his dramatic flair. "My father does not exaggerate on this. We truly miss my mother's baking."

"How is the stove working?" Mikolaj asked. "I remember that it came with the farm."

Marianna smiled. "The stove works well. It can burn both wood and coal. Since we moved here, I experimented with the controls. Every stove works a little differently."

"Marianna has practiced much." Andrzej emphasized, stepping forward and thrusting his hands on his hips. "Once she was confident about the operation of the stove, Marianna commanded all of us to stay away from it!"

Marianna felt a heat fill her cheeks. She looked across the room at the faces. *Are they laughing at my expense?* He had not said something untrue, but still, she did not like when he did this. Before Marianna could think of an appropriate retort, her father stepped forward and spoke.

"Marianna and Helena, tell them what you have planned to keep Antoni warm."

Helena locked her round eyes onto each visitor in turn as she began to describe their efforts. "This fall, Nikodimas and Andrzej cut and hauled, oh so many trees and tree falls, until we feared their backs would break!"

"The previous owner did not leave any wood?" Mikolaj asked.

"Just a few sticks," Andrzej replied. "The coal bin in the cellar was empty also. Nikodimas and I split much wood and filled the woodshed."

"The man who last owned this property was about sixty," Nikodimas explained. "He and his wife were alone here to deal with the farm."

"Perhaps they knew they would be leaving," Mikolaj said.

"That is probably so," Nikodimas agreed. "The wood did not cost us much—just sore muscles and a few blisters. The good wood in the pile may be too green still by winter. It concerns me. We have discussed using coal in the stove."

Andrzej did not say anything.

"You must have incurred many expenses with the purchase of the property." Mikolaj nodded, indicating he understood the situation. "Well, burning wood is a practical choice on this property—though your logic, Nikodimas, is insightful and worth further deliberation amongst you. Coal does offer an even, long fire that does not need tending so often."

"And far less ash to haul!" Nikodimas commented with a grin.

"Well, like many things in life, benefits have a price," Mikolaj suggested.

Andrzej rolled his eyes. "We have talked about this since Antoni's birth."

"Whatever we decide," Marianna stressed, "could save or harm our newest son." She paused, and then rested her eyes on Savetta, then Sally, and then Helena, who were now sitting on the kitchen sofa. "The thickest pieces of the new oak will be a good choice if they are dry enough not to smoke. We are most concerned about the night. It is a difficult balance—to get long lasting embers that remain at a comfortable heat."

"Marianna, how much will you wrap the baby?" Savetta asked.

"That will be part of what we will test carefully, Savetta. When Antoni is stronger, we will use layers of different fabric and place him in the basket Andrzej wove. Helena and I will try short times at first." Marianna looked at Mikolaj, waiting for him to appreciate that she had extended a compliment in place of the barb they might have expected.

"This sturdy basket makes me think of our village in the old country," Mikolaj Bychkowsky recollected.

"In the spring, when the hazelnut switches are most pliable, Mikolaj, I plan to make more baskets. I will remember to give you one."

"Then what will you do?" Eight-year-old Sally burst out. "With the baby!"

All heads turned to the little girl. Nellie and Michal giggled, with hands over their mouths.

Sally's father blushed. He did encourage her to listen well and think about things.

Mikolaj Bychkowsky sheepishly looked over at Andrzej and Marianna, then at his wife.

Before anyone could scold Sally for interrupting an adult conversation, Helena wrapped her arm around the girl, pulling her close. "Shall I show you what we will do next?" Sally shook her head up and down vigorously.

Marianna narrated while the midwife pantomimed the process. Helena opened the oven door, and then dragged the end table they would use in front of the stove. She tucked a green wool afghan loosely around an imaginary baby. Then, she placed the bundle in the basket, and the basket on the table.

"Helena knit this miniature afghan, some booties, and even a tiny hat just for Antoni," Marianna noted. "They are a beautiful green, like the leaves on a lilac bush in spring. The yarn was a gift from Helena's aunt when we moved to the farm."

"Marianna, I was pleased to knit them. They will help the baby to stay warm." Helena turned and tilted her head. "Sally, can you imagine Antoni in this basket?"

"Yes! I can see him," exclaimed the girl, as her parents stood by speechless.

"Over the next few months, Marianna and I intend to vary the amount of wood, and maybe try coal also. We will test the heat on ourselves first, and then place Antoni in the basket for more minutes each time, during the day and at night, being careful to ensure that Antoni stays warm, but not too warm, especially as the weather grows colder and we need to adjust the stove controls some. When Antoni is strong enough to leave his mother's chest, we will be ready."

Suddenly little Sally seemed distressed. "This will not cook the baby, will it?"

"Enough child," Savetta cautioned in a gentle whisper.

Helena waited a moment, and then spoke to the girl. "Do not worry little one. Have you ever seen baby chicks kept warm in the oven after they have hatched in the springtime?"

Sally slunk back. "Are you trying to fool me?"

Bernice L. Rocque

Her father bent down and reassured his daughter that some farmers had great success with this warming method.

Helena turned her head and blinked in apology to the parents, before explaining to their daughter, "We will heat the oven differently than for the chicks, but we will make sure that Antoni is not too warm."

"It seems you have given this much thought already," Savetta commented. "I have one suggestion, if you are interested."

"Of course," Marianna implored. "Savetta, please tell us what you are thinking."

"Have you considered inserting small pieces of moistened cotton in the spaces between the basket's weave?"

"Oh! To help Antoni breathe easier," Marianna thought out loud. "We will discuss that further. Thank you for mentioning this."

Savetta drew Sally closer and smiled at Marianna.

"I wish to learn more about this next time we see you." Savetta stood, then walked over and touched Marianna's arm gently, lowering her voice so that just Marianna could hear,

"Any family can have a small baby. It is good to know."

"Well, we have stayed far too long," Mikolaj announced with a lilt of his head towards Andrzej, and then Marianna, as he heard the chimes of the clock. "I beg your forgiveness, but the conversation has been most thought provoking. The sun is rising and we must go, or I will be late for work."

"No need to apologize, Mikolaj," replied Andrzej. "You are always welcome and we hope you will stop by again soon."

After the Bychkowsky family left, Helena and Nikodimas reverted to speaking Polish, the language of the household. How juicy the roasted chickens would be! What else might they prepare? Oh, they could bring up some sweet potatoes from the root cellar and white potatoes too. Maybe a yellow turnip, some carrots, and a small bunch of onions would be tasty!

Marianna looked over at Andrzej who had followed the animated conversation with pride in his eyes, the generosity of his relatives having started this discussion.

Bernice L. Rocque

"Helena, you prepare the most delicious chicken of anyone we know," he exclaimed. "We look forward to the meal tonight."

"Thank you, Andrzej. If you think the cheese you were straining the other day is ready, I could make some pierogi as well."

"The cheese is ready, Helena. Please take what you need." Everyone loved the large dumplings, filled with the dry, finely textured cheese, and served warm slathered in heavy cream. Nellie looked at Michal. With both eyebrows raised, she whispered something in her brother's ear.

"Helena, would you also make a stuffing for the chickens if I crack some nuts and break up some of the older bread?" As Nikodimas spoke, he noticed that Nellie and Michal were eager to ask a question.

"Yes, my little ones, you can help me," to which the two children jumped up, hugged each other, and then danced in a circle until they fell on the floor laughing.

For a little while, even Marianna forgot to worry about the tiny baby boy who lay quietly on her chest.

Chapter Six

On the morning after their sumptuous chicken dinner, Helena got up earlier than usual. She made four loaves of bread and a large pot of Venison stew, finishing off the deer meat. Already the first of December, it was time to register the birth. Since it was Friday, she would stop at City Hall on her way home. She wanted to bathe, get some fresh clothes, and prepare some food for her husband. After nearly ten years of marriage, he was used to her disappearing for days when she was midwifing. Still, she did not like to be away for too long.

Before Helena left, she talked with Andrzej and Marianna, writing down the correct information for the office of the City Clerk. Andrzej asked Helena to ensure that "Anthony," the American spelling of their son's name, was recorded on the form.

Since the birth, the family had many heated discussions about getting Antoni baptized, with voices raised on occasion. At one point, Nikodimas had deflected an argument. "Ah," he had noted, "the priest will drive all the way out to the country to bless bread, but not to baptize a fragile infant." Even Andrzej shook his head in frustration.

The Church taught that parents should baptize newborns as soon as was reasonably possible. Neither of Antoni's parents wanted to dwell on the frightening thought that their newest son might expire before receiving the sacrament and spend eternity in limbo. But, taking such a tiny infant out into the December air also seemed unwise. In the end, it was Helena who made the most sense to everyone.

"Have we not put our faith in the Blessed Mother and in St. Michal?" she asked. "Then, we need to trust."

They would make the trip to the church. But which church? Andrzej wanted to have his son baptized at St. Joseph's, the Polish church downtown. Marianna had confided to Helena that she favored Sacred Heart Church in Norwichtown, less than two miles from the farm, even though this nearby parish did not have a Polish priest like St. Joseph's, where they felt more comfortable.

Seven chimes of the clock reminded Helena that she needed to be on her way.

"Marianna, should I talk with the priest at Sacred Heart?"

"Antoni will be baptized at St. Joseph's," Andrzej interjected as he stepped into the kitchen from the sitting room. He stopped and stared into Helena's surprised face and added, "Helena, would you honor Marianna and me by becoming godmother for our second son?"

Helena bowed her head slightly in deference to the head of the household, but waited for confirmation from her friend who did not move or speak at first. When Marianna looked up, Helena detected that her friend had ceded to her husband's wishes.

"My dear friend Helena, it would mean so much if you will be godmother for Antoni." The midwife was relieved to sense calm in Marianna's voice.

Helena bent toward Marianna, and then smiled. "Of course, I would be proud to be godmother again, and especially for Antoni who seems protected by the love of the Blessed Mother."

"Her feast day is soon."

"Yes," Helena said, hearing the hope in her friend's voice. The midwife could not help smiling just a little. "It does seem a fortuitous time for his baptism, Marianna."

"May I say, Helena, that your face radiates your deep faith, and this faith has helped us so much," Andrzej emphasized.

"I feel certain that the Blessed Mother is watching over this baby," Helena said. "Each day that Antoni lives, I am convinced more that he has been saved for a reason. Perhaps someday we will learn why."

"Perhaps he will save one of us someday!" Nikodimas sang out, having caught the end of the conversation as he strode into the kitchen from the outside.

Andrzej took a loud deep breath, pursed his lips, and resumed his conversation with the midwife. "Helena, could you speak with

Jan Sak? We hope he will honor us by becoming godfather for Antoni, and also drive us to the church Sunday. If so, please go ahead and talk with the priest at St. Joseph's."

Helena nodded. "I will return late Saturday afternoon. God willing, the winter wind will stay away until after this joyous occasion."

Helena embraced Andrzej, then Nikodimas, and finally Marianna. As she turned to leave, Andrzej grabbed Helena's wrist. "Please—take this for the streetcar."

"Thank you, Andrzej." She dropped the dime into the pocket of her smock, put on her long wool coat and draped the folded scarf over her head, tying it under her chin.

"Helena, if you are ready to go, I can walk with you to the trolley." Nikodimas put his arms through the sleeves of his winter coat and pulled a wool cap from his pocket.

"What a nice surprise! Your company is most welcome."

Marianna stood suddenly, clutching Antoni to her. "Father, when will you return?" she asked in Lithuanian.

Bernice L. Rocque

"I will be back for supper," he replied in Lithuanian. "Please be sure to save me a generous bowl of Helena's wonderful venison stew!"

With a big grin on his face, Nikodimas danced towards the door with Helena on his arm. They crossed the yard and started down the dirt road, talking as they went and waving or stopping briefly to chat with neighbors who happened to be outside. As they headed down the last two hills near the bottom of the street, they were able to talk uninterrupted.

"Nikodimas, thank you for your kind words about my stew."

"You are welcome, Helena. We could not have gotten through this week without your help, but surely you must be exhausted."

"Yes, it has been a long week for all of us. But it is a good feeling to know that Antoni lives, at least for the moment. Marianna has been so relieved that you have been home this past week, Nikodimas."

"My daughter, Marianna, is smart like her mother. She expects it is time I talk with the Russian."

"Marianna worries about these trips the two of you make to Brooklyn."

"I know, Helena. I am careful, though the danger is not too great. The citizens of America," he whispered, "do not seem to support this law about liquor. Even the police do not want to enforce it. Most have their hands out and we are happy to oblige. This makes each trip less risky."

"How can you depend that everyone feels the same?" Helena lowered her head and her voice. "Nikodimas, forgive me for being so outspoken. I know it is not my business. Perhaps we should change the subject."

"Helena, I believe you are a dear friend who is concerned. Please, empty your heart. I will listen."

Helena wondered how this man could be so different from most. How fortunate Marianna was to have him as her father. He made everyone feel important and comfortable.

"Marianna worries much about many things. You know this, Nikodimas. But, about this I feel she has good reason. There may be some who will want to trap you, the Russian, and the others. Have you thought about how this would affect Marianna and Andrzej, and of course, the children?"

"What can I say, Helena? Without this business our family would still be living downtown, though High Street was nicer than some places we lived in America. Instead, we own a farm. And, God willing, we will own the land across from us in a few years, and I will convince my Paulina to join us here."

Helena knew the story about the house that he had built for his wife in Lithuania before he left. How happy his wife had been when they moved into it. Marianna said it had helped her mother to veil the tragedies of the other house, the house near the river, where two of her sons had drowned.

"This separation from your wife must be difficult."

"Yes, but I am crazy for this country. I have crossed the ocean a few times and traveled all around America. I described to Paulina what I saw each time. It is difficult for some people to let go. She would not leave her family, and of course the new house, unless she was certain there was something much better in America." He laughed loudly. "I think most people feel I am persuasive, but my Paulina is unconvinced so far."

Helena smiled. "Perhaps you and Jan Sak commiserate sometimes?"

"We might, except that Jan has no desire to see his wife again. They did not agree on very much, but he was still hurt when she decided to return to Poland. Some marriages work out happily. Others do not."

"Nikodimas, do you not believe that you and Andrzej could have worked at regular jobs and saved the money in a few years for a farm like this, or maybe a smaller one at first?"

"Dearest Helena, you are so like a daughter to me. The families on this street are not really wealthy, but many have owned their property for generations. Remember, I have less time. I have seen how things work."

"In what way, Nikodimas? I do not understand."

"I am not complaining really. When I had to stay in America longer than I expected during the Great War, I found work in a

Bernice L. Rocque

respected gun factory. You remember—they even made me a boss."

"And you used your skill from the old country. Not everyone is able to do that."

"Yes, that is true. I earned more than most employees there, but still, not very much, considering all the different things I did. When I left the job, they gave me a shotgun and a violin, thanking me for my toil, effort, and good humor. Hah!"

"You did not feel appreciated?"

He stopped walking, tilted his head, and reached out his arms toward Helena. "I did fine metal work, interpreted, mediated at times, and kept the employees happy and productive."

"Ah. I understand. So that the owners could take home most of the profit."

The air filled with their rollicking snorts as they descended the final hill to the Bean Hill green.

"One cannot argue with what you have said, Nikodimas. I admire your courage. Tell me, what does the Russian call you when you are working together?"

"I am 'the musician.'" His blue eyes sparked with pleasure. "We take the violin on every trip to Brooklyn, in case we are stopped. The Russian depends on me to spin a story and explain in English, if it is needed." The amusement in his voice did not escape his companion. *These trips were about more than the money.* His buoyant spirit and the hearty laugh that drew his beloved family to him also disarmed his adversaries. Nikodimas was a man of many faces.

"It is wonderful that things come so easily to you, Nikodimas. Well, we have timed this well. The trolley must be on this side of Yantic. I can just hear the bells. Do you hear them?"

"The gun factory took away a pinch of my hearing. It is a minor inconvenience!"

"A mile goes by quickly when you have good company and good conversation. Thank you for walking with me."

Nikodimas bowed like an actor on the stage. "Helena, you are like a member of our family. I so appreciate the love and wisdom you have brought to our household. Andrzej and Marianna will have other gifts for you, I am sure, but please accept this from the grandfather of Antoni."

Before she could refuse, he pushed a ten dollar bill into her hand, and the two rushed across the street to board the streetcar.

Chapter Seven

When Jan Sak arrived at the farm at nine o'clock on Sunday morning, the third of December, his friends were waiting for him. He parked in front of the house, just steps from the front door, leaving the engine running so the car was nicely heated when Helena slid into the narrow back seat and Andrzej helped Marianna into the front seat. Once Andrzej squeezed into the back seat next to Helena, Marianna opened the top part of her coat, so that Jan could catch a glimpse of little Antoni.

"Oh, what a handsome boy he is! Yes, he is small, but do not worry. He will grow big and strong. After all, he has survived already ten days."

"Jan, we thought our new son was doing very well," Andrzej confided.

"What happened, Andrzej? Oh no! Did Antoni have a setback?"

Bernice L. Rocque

"No, no. Dr. Thompson visited yesterday to verify Antoni's birth. He looked at Antoni and said nothing at first. He examined him, weighed him, and asked Marianna questions about whether Antoni was feeding and so forth. Then, he stood back and said to Marianna, 'This is the smallest baby I ever saw—dead or alive.'"

"Oh! Andrzej, I am sure he did not mean to be unkind. He spoke before he thought," Jan said in a consoling voice.

"That is not all, Jan," Andrzej stammered. "When he saw Marianna's reaction, he took us aside, Nikodimas and I, and told us that babies weighing less than three pounds usually die in the first few weeks, and we should prepare the mother. Of course, Marianna has ears like a bunny rabbit and she heard him say these unspeakable words."

"Yes, I heard the doctor say these things, Jan. I am sure he is right. Many small babies die, but some live, God willing."

"I have a feeling about this, Marianna. I am sure things will turn out fine."

The gentle confidence she heard in Jan's voice made her feel calmer.

"Well, shall we get going down the street?" Jan asked, smiling at Marianna, then Helena, then Andrzej.

"Yes, Jan," urged Andrzej. "We should be on our way."

They waved goodbye to Nikodimas and the children, whose noses and fingers were pressed against the window panes in the front parlor. Jan engaged the car and started down the dirt road.

"Jan, your words about Antoni are welcome to our ears," Andrzej commented. "They were far kinder than the doctor's. We are doing everything we know how to do."

Hearing the frustration in her husband's voice, Marianna added, "Jan, everyone has helped—Helena, Andrzej, and my father, so that I have been able to hold Antoni close to me and warm him since he was born."

Marianna leaned back, comfortable with her infant against her chest. She appreciated the effort Jan took with his driving, maneuvering the automobile slowly down the

Bernice L. Rocque

first few hills of the bumpy dirt road. When they reached the level middle section of the street, the prospective godfather started up the conversation again.

"Yes, Antoni is a lucky boy. I wish he could talk to us, Marianna. Do you wonder what Antoni understands?"

"When it is quiet, Jan, and I am sitting with him, I stroke his cheek lightly and whisper songs to him. So many things go through my head. Most of all I think—if he can hear my heart beating, like he did before he was born, our Antoni will feel safe, and maybe that comfort will keep him with us." She closed her eyes for a moment and breathed in deeply.

"Marianna, Andrzej, Helena, I am so sorry that the doctor does not have faith like we do. Please do not worry. Antoni is eating, is he not? And, he is doing all the messy things that newborns do, yes?"

Andrzej, Marianna, and Helena burst out. It felt good to laugh, until Antoni began to cry. Marianna waved her arm and everyone became silent as she comforted her son.

A few minutes later when Antoni had settled down, Jan whispered, "Marianna, I am so sorry to be the cause of Antoni becoming frightened."

"Please do not feel badly. I can never be angry with you, Jan."

"I am so glad, Marianna."

"Jan, you always make us laugh," Helena added. "This week, especially, we need to laugh, and it is good for Antoni to hear happy voices."

"Yes, happy voices!" Jan sang. "Has everyone noticed that we have a nice sunny day to drive to the church? It is as beautiful as a poem. That is a hint, Marianna, about the surprise I have brought for you. In Lithuania, people sing more often. I know you miss the song."

While Jan navigated down the serpentine curves of the largest hill, swerving gently to avoid ruts that could cause them difficulty, Marianna bubbled with anticipation.

After coming to a stop at the bottom of the street, Jan reached into a compartment and handed Marianna an unsealed envelope.

Bernice L. Rocque

"What is this, Jan?" With only one hand free, Marianna fumbled with her thumb and forefinger to spread the opening of the envelope.

"I know how much you enjoy poems, so I cut them from my friend's Lithuanian newspaper. Maybe their song will chase your worry away."

"You drive us and bring laughter and poems, Jan, and Helena sewed me a blouse satchel when she went home Friday to make it easier to hold Antoni close to me while I walk. You are both such wonderful friends."

"We are truly blessed," echoed Andrzej.

The four talked away during the next five miles to their destination. The traveling was good and the trip took less than thirty minutes. On the way, Andrzej pointed out the Norwich Free Academy.

"Someday Antoni will attend this fine school, and we will all be proud."

Marianna reflected that this was one subject about which her husband and her father agreed.

By mid-morning, Antoni had a godmother and godfather, and the blessing of the sacrament of baptism. The Polish priest kept the ceremony brief, and all were relieved that Antoni slept through it. On the ride home, Marianna supported her son against her chest. Her arm felt light like air. The tension that had plagued her entire body for days was missing. Marianna closed her eyes. She was certain that if anything happened to her or to Andrzej, these two good friends would look after and love this child.

Bernice L. Rocque

Chapter Eight

On Christmas Eve, Nikodimas and his two grandchildren walked past the barn. They followed the winding path down to the lower pasture, the children chattering about Santa most of the way, their voices filling the crisp air with their hopes and expectations. The three soon disappeared into the woods, just like the stone wall to their left that ran the length of the path.

Ahead, fallen leaves cloaked much of the hilly terrain. For every rock that jutted out, Nikodimas surmised that surely three were hidden. A few yards up the gentle slope Nellie stopped.

"I see a little tree!" Nellie pointed and began to run, the thin forest around her darkening and brightening as clouds passed in front of the midday sun.

"Be careful, little one," her grandfather shouted, shaking his head, both bemused and concerned. "The ground might be slippery." The rain a few days earlier had melted most of the December snow.

Nikodimas grabbed Michal's hand and the two followed his granddaughter.

Nellie glided around the tree twice. "Dziadzia, do you like it? Is this tree beautiful enough for our Christmas?"

"Well, Nellie, may I ask you to hold onto your brother's hand while I inspect this proud little tree?"

"Yes, Dziadzia." Nellie giggled. "How do you know it is proud?" She stood with her hand on her hip, waiting for an answer.

"Ah, well. See how the little tree stands straight and tall! That is how you can tell it is confident."

"I can reach most of the branches. See, Dziadzia." Nellie raised her free arm and looked up at her grandfather.

"I can see that you have grown much since last summer. Yes, your mother and father will think this is a very good tree. Not too tall. Not too fat. It will fit nicely in the sitting room."

Bernice L. Rocque

"Oh, Michal!" Nellie hugged her brother, and then at her grandfather's request, pulled the two-year-old back a few steps from the little tree.

"Are you going to cut it down with the saw, Dziadzia? Will it hurt the tree?"

"All of us return to the Lord sometime, Nellie. I brought the saw and the shovel. This year, we will use the shovel and try to keep the tree alive. If it survives, we will plant it this spring where it will get more sunlight."

He knelt and dug less than a minute. The roots of the tiny Norway spruce were shallow, as he expected. Nikodimas lifted the tree with ease from the soil and wrapped the roots gently with a rag that he had moistened at the house.

Before standing up, he cupped his ear and twisted toward the children. "Did you hear what the little tree said?"

Michal and Nellie peered at their grandfather.

"No," said Nellie. Scrunching her face, she said to her grandfather, "Is the little tree really talking to you?"

"Trees have much to say. This one is telling me it feels honored to spend Christmas with our family."

"Dziadzia, I did not hear you speak to the tree."

"I did not speak to it. One can learn much when one listens."

Nellie dug her toe into the leaves on the ground. Realizing her grandfather was waiting for her reply, she suddenly stood up straight, her chin extended out toward her grandfather.

"Michal and I are listening now."

"What do you hear?"

Nellie giggled and looked up. "I think the tree is saying, 'Take me home right away!'"

Nikodimas stifled a laugh and put his hand to the back of his ear again. "Oh! The little tree has more to say."

"You are funny, Dziadzia."

"The little tree is very happy that you noticed it when you came into the forest."

"I love the little tree. What do you think, Michal?"

Her brother ran his hand through the branches of the tree. "Pretty tree, Dziadzia."

Bernice L. Rocque

"This is good. We will all love the little tree and will decorate it today with fine ornaments. Someday, Nellie, we will remember that you found this beautiful tree on our first Christmas here at the farm."

Nikodimas grabbed the base of the tree trunk and they started home, the children running ahead of him. When he reached the farmhouse, he set the base of the trunk in a bucket, filled it with sand from the pile behind the gray shed, and slowly added a few quarts of water from the well. Inside the house, he found that everyone was talking at once.

"So soon you are back." Marianna exclaimed. "Helena and I want to know," she teased, "how did you find such a friendly tree?"

Nikodimas and Nellie blinked at each other.

"Your daughter spotted the tree right away, Marianna."

Nellie beamed, "Dziadzia said the tree was waiting for us to find it."

"Ah, so it was meant to be," Helena chimed in.

"So it seems!" Nikodimas agreed playfully. "But, I think we will save a discussion about fate for another time, maybe on a day when the snow reaches the windowpanes—if winter ever arrives. Hah! How can I help with the Wigilia preparations?"

"Thank you for asking, Father. Helena has already swept the house and changed the bed linens. We could use the extra table now, the one with the two leaves, and some clean straw from the barn to put under our tablecloth. Oh—and some evergreen clippings for the tops of the two tables."

"Yes, these are customary and easy tasks for me, Marianna. I know there is more to do and I see tiredness in your face. Antoni is getting stronger but he still needs most of your attention."

"Father, you know how I love Christmas Eve! But, I have anticipated your concern. Helena and I are trying to keep the preparations as simple as possible. She peels, cuts and chops, and I stir. We work well together."

Bernice L. Rocque

"Certainly, there are other things I can do to help. The children and I could decorate the tree, if it is acceptable. When do you expect Andrzej to return from the work he got last week?"

"He told me about four o'clock. Helena's husband, Mike, and Jan Sak should arrive by five. Andrzej will want us to wait for our guests, even if the first star in the sky has appeared."

"Yes, of course we will wait. Jan is always gracious. And I do not think Mike will mind either. After all, he adopted an American nickname almost as soon as he walked off the boat."

"Father, I have been thinking while you were talking. Our work in the kitchen will be easier if the children are occupied in the sitting room. When you are ready, the box of ornaments is in the parlor."

"Good! I am glad to be of more help."

"Will you put aside a few ornaments, Father? The children and my husband can place them on the tree when he returns."

"I will, Marianna."

Nikodimas headed out to the barn to retrieve the extra table. That afternoon, the household bustled with activity, including baths for everyone, as was the Lithuanian tradition. By the time Mike and Jan arrived, Andrzej had changed into clean clothes and welcomed the two men at the front door.

Mike presented Andrzej with a gift of apricot brandy, to a chorus of approving "oohs" and "ahs."

"Dziekuje, Mike. This is a delicious favorite for our Wigilia toast. Marianna has said often that the color reminds her of the amber that is plentiful in Lithuania."

Andrzej fetched six shot glasses from the glass hutch in the parlor, opened the bottle, and poured the orange-gold colored liqueur, handing the filled glasses out as he went.

Standing in the entryway between the two rooms, Andrzej raised his glass to everyone in the crowded kitchen. "Na zdrowie."

The five other adults lifted their glasses and repeated the toast to good health. Both men and women downed the brandy in one swallow. After that, the light and shadows thrown by the kerosene lantern seemed softer as the women returned to preparing the meal and the men lingered in the kitchen talking.

"It is taking all my willpower not to scoop up some of the turnip," Helena whispered to Marianna as she mashed the vegetable.

Nikodimas, standing closest to the two women, began to listen to their conversation. He had expressed concern earlier that day when he learned that Helena had decided to do her usual Wigilia fasting.

Marianna leaned towards her friend's ear. "Helena, you look pale. Are you feeling poorly?"

Nikodimas continued to listen, interested in what Helena would reply to his daughter. He nodded as if he had understanding about something Andrzej was saying to Jan.

"Just tired. And hungry!" Helena sighed and then chuckled.

"If you are feeling faint, please do not be foolish," Marianna implored. "Eat a small bite of something."

Nikodimas decided not to intrude on the conversation. Marianna would keep a close watch on her friend until they sat down to dinner. Perhaps Helena would heed his daughter's advice. If hunger was gnawing at Helena's insides and waves of nausea were possibly washing over her, he knew why this was happening. Helena's exhaustion was catching up to Marianna's.

"I almost forgot," Jan said, handing Marianna the bag he was holding. "Maybe this will be the twelfth dish for our Wigilia." He gave her a broad smile and then asked, "Where are the children? Are they hiding?"

Helena crooked her finger, pointing it toward the back of the sitting room. "Forgive me, Jan," Marianna pleaded. "I will open your gift in a few minutes. These potatoes need tending or they will be mush."

"Jan," Nikodimas said in a low voice, "to answer your question, the children have been lying under the tree pretending they are outside in the forest where the little tree was."

Despite his attempt at whispering, Nellie apparently heard. She slid out from under the tree and ran into the kitchen, with Michal tagging along behind her. Jan gripped her waist and lifted her high off the floor. Michal

Bernice L. Rocque

raised his arms, hoping for the same, and Jan obliged as usual.

"You are both getting much heavier!" Jan commented.

"That was fun, Jan." Nellie cooed, as she grabbed his hand. "Come and see our Christmas tree and our stockings for Santa."

"Marianna," Jan called, getting her attention and pointing over the shoulders to the bag he had given her. "I ordered these at Bokoff's to make sure they saved some for me."

Before Marianna could look inside the paper bag, Nellie pulled Jan into the sitting room. Andrzej, Nikodimas, and Mike followed. They all stood in front of the little Christmas tree. Metallic garlands and glass ornaments of many colors sparkled in the lantern light.

"Who decorated the tree so artistically?" Jan asked.

Nellie grinned. "Dziadzia, my brother, Michal, and I—and my Tata," she announced, looking up at her father who was nodding.

"Well, this is just the most beautiful tree I have ever seen," Jan exclaimed.

"Jan. Oh, Jan," Marianna exclaimed as she appeared in the entryway to the sitting room, her right hand cupping Antoni against her body. "You brought us smelts for our Wigilia!"

"I thought you would like to have them."

"We have been so occupied, Jan. This afternoon, it was making me sad when I realized there would be no fish on our Wigilia table."

"Marianna, you need not have worried about this. It would have been fine. Taking care of Antoni has been far more important than anything else. Everyone understands. I assure you."

Marianna leaned over and gave Jan a big kiss on one cheek, and then the other. "Thank you for bringing this fish for our Wigilia dinner. And the oil!"

"I knew you would rather not use butter or lard on Christmas Eve."

."You remembered how much I love smelts, Jan. Well, if your nose is working well tonight, I think you can tell that Helena has started to cook the smelts in the fresh oil."

Bernice L. Rocque

"I can! I look forward to eating a few."

"All the Wigilia aromas are making me hungry, Marianna," Mike prodded.

"Supper will be ready in a few minutes, Mike."

"Marianna, I have not heard a peep from Antoni," Jan whispered. "How is he doing?"

Marianna lifted Antoni higher, showing him to Jan and Mike.

"We are both doing well, better than anyone expected. My Antosh is a quiet baby. He is almost a pound bigger since you drove us to St. Joseph's. But, each morning, Jan, I start out the same—so afraid. I cannot help it. When I touch his shoulder and find that he is still with us, I think I must be dreaming. He is not breastfeeding yet, but the eye dropper that Helena gave us is working well."

"Who is Helena?" Mike joked. They all roared with laughter. Marianna smiled, shook her head, and returned to the kitchen.

"Surely you could not forget the beautiful face and culinary ability of your exceptional Polish woman," Andrzej teased. "How long have you been married, now?"

"Let me think about this." Mike played along, closing his eyes and lifting his chin. "Almost ten—"

The force of a resounding sneeze threw Mike's head back.

"Na zdrowie," Andrzej responded, his expression changing from amusement to concern. Without moving his head, he looked over at Nikodimas.

"With all seriousness," Nikodimas said, picking up the conversation, "on a night when we must be thankful, we thank you, Mike, for your sacrifice. Helena is an indispensible midwife and a true friend of our family. I am sure, though, that she has tired of looking at the walls of our kitchen!" Nikodimas chuckled.

"Yes, her commitment to this tiny child is unshakeable," Mike reflected. A slight frown appeared at the corner of his mouth. "Helena is a generous person, but she rarely dedicates herself like she has for Antoni and your family. If she did this for everyone, I would never see her!" He had tried to make light of it, but those listening could detect a tinge of resentment.

"My sincere apology to you, Mike," Andrzej offered. "It must be difficult to go back to being a bachelor when you are spoiled by the care of a good wife."

"Bachelor!" Mike bellowed. "I am more like a widower in the last month!"

The sitting room exploded in laughter. When Helena stuck her head into the room, asking what was so humorous, Mike's face reddened.

"It is just a lonely man's joke, Helena," Andrzej told her. She squinted at them and returned to the kitchen.

"I have come to appreciate how many things Helena does in our household," Mike continued. "People have taken pity on me, though, and invited me for meals."

"That is good to hear, Mike," Andrzej remarked.

"My wife and I will go home tonight and have our own Christmas. Tomorrow, we will visit with Helena's family and by the New Year our apartment will be clean and back in order."

A lull in the conversation followed. Nikodimas filled the quiet by asking the children what kinds of treats they planned to leave on Santa's plate. He watched the lively interchange with everyone guessing what might please Santa most.

When Marianna finally appeared in the entrance to the sitting room her father was relieved. She had toiled far too much during the day, but to his amazement, her face glowed. She reached out to everyone with her free arm, while steadying Antoni with the other.

"It is time for our Wigilia meal," she announced. "The twelve dishes are on the table in the kitchen. Please remember to take food from every dish and we will bring our plates to the table in the sitting room. There is a pitcher of hard cider and one with water there. Please take what you want."

Nellie strolled with her mother into the kitchen. The family and friends formed a circle around the table and slowly started to wind their way around the serving dishes. While Helena began to prepare plates for herself and Nellie, the little girl stood on her tiptoes. Nikodimas watched his granddaughter's eyes

Bernice L. Rocque

dart with delight across the dishes of carrots, pickled beets and onions, dark rye bread, boiled potatoes with dill, mashed turnip, applesauce, lima beans, pierogi, and smelts. A quizzical expression took over her face when her eyes reached the bowl of Kucia.

Nellie pointed to the dish. "What is that, Matka?"

"This is called Kucia," Marianna explained. "It is cereal. Your grandfather made the Kucia with barley, wheat, oats, honey, and poppy seed milk. In Lithuania where your grandfather and I used to live, Christmas Eve is called Kucios. The holy day is named after this food which Lithuanian and Polish people have eaten for hundreds of years."

"What is in the pierogi, Matka?"

"These pierogi are filled with cabbage, sauerkraut, and mushrooms. Your grandfather is probably licking his lips with anticipation. Helena has a way of cooking the stuffing until it is just singed and sweet."

"Dziadzia said there would be no meat."

"Yes, tonight is similar to Fridays," Marianna said, as Helena lifted a smelt to the two plates. "On Christmas Eve, we do not eat meat or food that we get from our animals. So, that means we try not to use milk, or cream, or cheese in the food. There is some, though, in the pierogi and the desserts. We are not as strict as some families about this."

"There is so much food, Matka. It smells good," the little girl said.

"Do you remember why Wigilia is a holy day, Nellie?"

"Tata told me. When we were putting ornaments on the tree. Wigilia means... Matka, I cannot remember."

"Do you remember the name of the Christmas baby?"

"Jesus Christ, our savior."

"Good!" Marianna praised. "Christmas is the birthday of Jesus. Because he is our savior, we bow our heads in respect when we say his name, like this. We celebrate Wigilia on the night before Christmas every year as we wait for Christmas to arrive. Wigilia means to keep a vigil—to wait."

Nellie beckoned her mother to come closer. "You will not tell Tata I forgot?"

Nikodimas turned his head, pretending that he did not hear.

"No, no. There is a lot to remember about Christmas Eve, and you are only four and a half. Each year you will remember more."

"Perhaps if you ask your Dziadzia tomorrow," Nikodimas hinted, "He will play some Christmas carols on his violin and we will sing about the birth of the baby Jesus."

Like her grandfather, Nellie bowed her head slightly, and then reached for a piece of rye bread for her plate.

"Marianna, the children and I had a fine conversation about Wigilia this afternoon while we decorated the tree."

"Yes, Matka. We talked about good manners." Nellie pursed her lips.

"Such as being silent once everyone is eating the meal," Nikodimas helped. "And Nellie asked thoughtful questions about our Wigilia traditions."

"That pleases me," Marianna commented, while looking down to check her tiny son.

As the circle of people moved a few steps, Nellie spied the two dishes of sweets.

Nikodimas could imagine the wheels turning in Nellie's head.

"Marianna, your children and I discussed what sometimes happens after dessert."

"Oh. The magic straw?" Marianna asked with a lilt in her voice.

"Yes, Matka!" Nellie exclaimed. "Dziadzia said we pull a piece of straw from under the tablecloth." The little girl squinted.

"Ah. This is a very old tradition." Nikodimas paused as he spooned some beets onto his plate. "It is believed that the length of the straw is a sign of how long a life that person will have."

Nellie's eyes widened just like they had that afternoon. Nikodimas noticed that others around the serving table were listening, too, the expressions reflecting perhaps memories of being Nellie's age and hearing this for the first time. When Nikodimas saw his granddaughter and Michal press their fingertips against the tablecloth, he did the same.

"I await your thoughts on the tablecloth," Nikodimas teased, while the other adults, including Andrzej, hid their amusement.

"It feels lumpy, Dziadzia." Nellie laughed.

"Lumpy," Michal mimicked and giggled. He looked up at his father who was adding lima beans to their two plates.

Nellie withdrew her hand carefully, trying not to collide with the arms and spoonfuls of food moving in all directions.

"Well, the good food on this table is more than half gone," Nikodimas prompted, his eyebrows raised and his head tipped in the usual signal to Nellie. "Our animals will get just a few morsels this year!"

"Oh! Matka, do the animals really talk on Christmas Eve?

"Yes, just like people, they say." Marianna responded in a serious tone.

"Of course, this is only after they feast on some of the leftovers from the Wigilia dinner!" Nikodimas reminded.

"Matka," Nellie urged, pulling on her mother's sleeve. "Matka, can we save some food for the animals?"

"People need to eat first, my dear daughter. If there is food left and your father gives his permission, you and your grandfather can make a trip to the barn if it is not too late."

Nikodimas watched as Nellie immediately closed her eyes and became very still. He chuckled. He could imagine her prayer and decided to silently join in. *Dear Lord, please save some food for the animals.*

"I think you can reach the dessert now, Nellie," her mother encouraged. "I know how much you and Michal like the Krustai. You will like the Kolachki, too. Helena made it."

Nellie quickly added one of each dessert to her plate and smiled up at her mother, and then Helena.

"The dough is sweet and filled with nuts," Helena said, just as Jan reached for a piece of the Kolachki. He complimented Helena and Marianna, again, on all the delicious looking dishes and the festive tables.

Once they were all seated for supper, Andrzej began with the sign of the cross and a blessing of gratitude for the good fortune of the year.

"We give thanks for this farm, our health, our newest son, the animals, the foodstuffs for the winter, and a Christmas Eve with family and good friends." After pointing to the single chair left empty at the table, Andrzej looked up to the heavens. "We welcome the spirits of any family members who have returned to the Lord in the past year and wish to join our gathering."

Looking at his daughter while he spoke, Andrzej told how Mary and Joseph could not find a place to stay in Bethlehem. "The straw under the tablecloth" he explained, "is a reminder each year that the baby Jesus was born in a stable, and that his parents received the shepherds and the three kings there. So, the extra chair also represents the willingness of those present tonight to receive unexpected visitors, should someone come to our door."

There were nods around the table. Then, everyone closed their eyes for a few moments of silent prayer and thanks.

Andrzej then asked his father-in-law, as the eldest in their family, to share the oplatek. Nikodimas wished Marianna, then Andrzej, then each person at the table a happy Christmas, as each broke off a piece of the wafer. While the thin pieces melted in their mouths, the family and guests closed their eyes in silent reverence.

As was traditional, there was little conversation while they ate, except at the start when Andrzej split the smelt on each child's plate and removed the long, spiny bone. Antoni, who had been changed and fed before the meal began, did not make a sound. Nikodimas saw the frown when Nellie swallowed the Kucia, but he was pleased that his granddaughter remembered this was a solemn meal and not the time for complaining. He smiled to himself. He had not liked the taste of the fermented cereal either when he was a child.

When a little food remained on most plates, the silence shattered.

Two gigantic sneezes erupted from Mike, whose face was thrust almost to his plate. While all the eyes at the table glued onto him, Mike took out a cotton handkerchief and blew three large honks.

"Na zdrowie," Andrzej said in a heavy breath as he looked over at his father-in-law.

Bernice L. Rocque

Nikodimas read the concern in Andrzej's face and in other faces around the table. In the eyes of his daughter, though, he saw terror.

Then, Antoni began to cry. Marianna's hand tightened against her satchel and she stood without thinking, forgetting the custom to remain seated until all were finished. She looked over at Helena, then at Jan, her mouth quivering.

"I will take Antoni into the kitchen. Perhaps he is hungry."

"I must be getting another cold," Mike explained. "Many were sick at work this week."

Jan laid his fork and knife down on his plate.

"It has been wonderful to spend Christmas Eve with you, Andrzej, and with you, Marianna, and with you, Nikodimas, and Nellie, and Michal." Jan paused. "And, with my dear friends, Helena and Mike. But, I think it is time to start home."

"Jan, we have not finished our meal of the twelve dishes," Mike protested. "You know it is bad luck if you do not taste each dish."

"Everyone is tired, Mike. Nellie and Michal are anxious to go to bed so that Santa can come and fill their stockings. It is best if we start home. It is not uncommon to be delayed by a flat tire. We all need to get a good night of sleep. After all, we are expected at our relatives tomorrow."

"I want to finish my meal." Mike insisted.

Before he could eat the remaining food on his plate, Helena pushed her chair back and stood up.

"I have enjoyed myself, but I am very tired and feel we need to travel home now. Nikodimas, please get our coats."

"Helena, I will bring the coats," Andrzej interceded.

Mike reluctantly followed his wife and Jan out the front door. Nikodimas walked with them to Jan's car and tried to smooth over the abrupt departure. When he returned inside, his jovial manner had disappeared.

"What did Mike say?" Andrzej pressed.

Nikodimas shrugged. "He said he would not visit the farm again."

Chapter Nine

It had been snowing since noon. The clock was chiming three and soon the daylight would be gone and the winter darkness would descend again. Marianna changed Antoni's diaper for the sixth time that day. She wrapped him with a clean white towel, adjusted his green booties and hat, and tucked the small afghan around him in his basket.

Marianna walked around the corner to the sitting room hutch and groaned as she bent over to open the bottom drawer. After lifting the top blouse, she discovered she could not stand without grabbing onto the wood trim around the entryway. *I feel like an old woman.* Marianna steadied herself for a moment, and while she did she noticed Helena's handiwork. *What a dear friend she is.* Marianna brushed the bottom of her hand across the fabric of the blouse. She hated that Helena was ironing these so frequently, but Helena had insisted.

"Your skin will be irritated enough. The ironing makes the fabric softer."

The day had opened with dark skies and heavy air. Everyone knew more snow was coming. Only a few weeks had passed since Christmas Eve, but to Marianna it seemed like months.

Once the January snows started, Helena had been washing mostly underwear, diapers, and Marianna's blouses which were drying on a rack in the sitting room. The midwife would bundle up, go outside early, and complete the chores that could not wait a day or two. Marianna had watched out the window as her friend traversed the icy paths, the lantern light shaking a strobe of patterns on the snow cover. When Helena came in, she would sit down for a while and close her eyes. She never complained to anyone about the difficulty of carrying out chores in the extreme weather. Instead, the midwife rested when she needed to rest. Marianna was grateful that Helena concentrated on being careful. It would not be good if she lost her footing while hauling water from the well or emptying chamber pots.

Early that morning, while donning his warmest coat and hat, Andrzej told them he would leave earlier for his job. He lit his work lantern, emptied the ash from the stove, overfilled the inside wood box, and then went below to the root cellar to bring up the items Helena wanted. She placed them on the counter, handed him a clean bucket for the milk, and inside it, a small basket for the eggs. Slipping the bucket handle over his wrist and grasping the outside door frame, he slowly pulled the door shut with the other hand, while backing down the three steps. Through the crocheted doily in the window of the door, the women observed Andrzej reach into the sand bucket outside and throw two handfuls on the steps, before heading down the illuminated snow path to the barn and the red shed.

Upon returning, Andrzej stood at the base of the steps and handed Helena the containers of milk and eggs. He tapped his boot edges on the rock near the well pump before coming in, and then sat with a thump. Marianna watched her husband eat a few pieces of bread with some cheese the midwife had melted for him.

Saying very little, he tied some rags around the tops of his boots, nodded to all, and walked out the front door. From the south window in the sitting room, the women shook their heads as he slogged down the snow covered road.

At least they did not need to worry about Marianna's father. Nikodimas had left the day before the last snowstorm, telling them that he would stay in Brooklyn with relatives if the weather was terrible.

It had been an exhausting morning. Marianna set the clean blouse on her chair, wishing she had felt up to helping. She removed the blouse she was wearing and hung it on the knob of the back door. Marianna dipped the wash cloth in the basin and squeezed out most of the water. The warmth of the water soothed her as she drew the cloth slowly under her arms and across her soiled chest. She emptied the used water into a chamber pot and filled the basin with a few inches of fresh water from the bucket and the tea kettle. Dipping and squeezing out the cloth again, Marianna dabbed and washed her breasts, removing remnants of dried milk.

When her skin was dry, she ran her fingertips across her chest. The stickiness was gone.

She picked up the fresh blouse, relieved that the ironed fabric would not chafe the front of her body, where everything was sensitive. After slipping her arms into the sleeves and fastening the buttons, Marianna stood closer to the stove, but held onto the wooden back of her chair while stretching each arm, and then shaking each stiff leg. Out of the corner of her eye, Marianna saw Helena observing her while kneading the bread they would eat at supper. Helena did not say a word, but just as Marianna turned towards her friend, Helena worked another handful of caraway seeds into the dough. The midwife shaped two long loaves of rye bread, placed them on a metal baking sheet, and put them in the oven. While cleaning her hands, Helena finally looked up.

"Marianna, you might try to get some sleep while the children and Antoni are napping. I will keep an eye on all of them while I prepare the vegetables for supper."

Marianna motioned that she had heard, and then settled her thin body on the kitchen sofa. Almost as soon as she closed her eyes, the room began to spin. She propped up the pillow behind her head, but could not find a position that relieved the vertigo.

"I am so tired of this."

"I know, Marianna. I can see that. You must remember—your sacrifice has helped Antoni to live."

"Perhaps," Marianna sighed. "I feel like I am in a different body."

Marianna rose and lumbered over to the kitchen chair in which she had spent countless hours. She adjusted the amount of recline in the back, and then tried again to doze while the house was quiet, but could not. There was no choice. She had to keep her eyes open for a while, and just sit there.

Glancing back and forth between the two windows in the kitchen was a bad choice, she soon remembered. Like the last time, her eye movement stoked the dizziness. Marianna gripped the arm of the chair, holding her breath for several seconds and looking straight ahead. Then, she gradually shifted her eyes to the south window, while slowly exhaling.

Outside, the falling snow, dense as fog, was shrouding the house like the blanket she was pulling closely around her. Four inches of snow sat in a narrow column on the railing of the side porch. Marianna wondered how much taller the column would get before it could not support itself any longer—and plummeted to the ground.

The foot-deep path from the back door to the porch steps, shoveled after every snowstorm so they could get to the stacked wood, was filling quickly with the new snow. The path's sharp edges were gone, sculpted into soft mounds by the wind. To the far right, the sweeping arms of the giant Norway spruce drooped like wilting white lilies.

"The snow is still coming," Marianna mumbled.

"Well, it is the second week of January," Helena said. "I was fortunate to return between the snows."

"It will be a long walk up the street for Andrzej."

"Yes, I am sure his feet will be frozen by the time he arrives home."

"And once he warms himself some, he will go back out and shovel the long paths."

Helena walked over to her friend.

"Marianna, do not worry about Andrzej. You have not eaten much today."

"I am not hungry."

"Our Antosh is growing nicely," Helena remarked, as she leaned toward Marianna. "It would not be good if his mother becomes ill."

"The food is not appealing."

"You are nauseous, I know. It is the fatigue that is causing this. I will make you some ginger tea and later, I want you to eat a few bites of bread."

"I will try."

"When your father returns from Brooklyn, I will ask him to buy a few chickens, so I can make you some broth and weak vegetable soup, with a little barley perhaps."

"Helena, we have chickens."

"I will let you think about whether you want to ask your father or Andrzej to chase a chicken around in this weather, Marianna. It does not seem the best idea to encourage either man to wield a hatchet. Both are tired."

Bernice L. Rocque

"Of course you are right, Helena. We love our Antosh, but no one, except my tiny son, has slept well since he arrived!"

"That is true, but we are strong. Our ancestors suffered much in Poland and Lithuania under the yoke of others, but still survived. It is now a while since we left our homes in the old country and came to America. We are doing fine. I think Antoni has the strength of our people in his bones and the love of the Blessed Mother protecting him. He has doubled his birth weight in six weeks."

"Three pounds is still small, Helena. It is difficult to forget what the doctor said."

"We must have faith, Marianna. Our Antosh is not as tiny as he was."

*   *   *

A week later, Helena went home for a few days. Before she returned to the farm, she bought more ginger root, some peppermint tea, and another chicken that was ready to cook.

After nearly two weeks of consuming chicken broth, mashed vegetables, and lightly buttered noodles, Marianna was able to tolerate soft chicken, so Helena began to cook everything from chicken soup to chicken stew for their meals. Marianna marveled at what Helena could get out of one chicken!

"I was surprised when you returned so quickly, Helena. I thought Mike might object."

"He did, but not for long. He can tell when he is wasting words. I would never forgive myself if something happened to you while you were weak."

"I am feeling much better. We are so grateful for your help, Helena. I thank the Lord every day that you are my friend."

"It is good to be useful, Marianna."

"I have said my rosary of thanks today and have helped to make our noon meal. Helena, are you concerned about me still?"

"Marianna, now that you are eating again and a little stronger, and everyone is at Mass, I will tell you what has been on my mind."

"Look, Helena, Antoni sleeps in his basket near the stove."

"Yes, Antoni is progressing." Helena made the sign of the cross and pressed her lips together.

"Helena, there is a troubled look in your face."

"Yes."

"What is it?"

"Marianna, it is time. He is more than two months old. We need to leave him in his basket overnight so that you can get better sleep. My saying this should not surprise you. We have discussed this much since Christmas. You promised to begin this in mid-January, but we did not. Of course, I understand that you were overcome with tiredness."

"He is still so small, Helena."

"Antoni is small yet, but he is acting like a full-sized baby. He is breathing normally, he is feeding well, and he is digesting the milk. The diapers are telling us that!"

"Yes, I am thankful for all these things."

"Marianna, we have all contributed to Antoni's survival, but, as your midwife, I must tell you that though you feel stronger today, if you continue to deprive yourself of sleep, I fear you could have a setback. I do not want that to happen. It could be serious. You would not be the first woman to love her child too much."

"There is more you want to say, Helena?"

"I think you are not convinced."

"Helena, I am getting three hours of sleep some nights—and I nap. You know that."

"Your body has been telling you it is not enough."

"I am feeling stronger."

"Marianna. How many times in the last month have you been unable to sleep, even though you were exhausted—and unable to eat, even though your body needed food? Everyone in the family has been fearful, including the children. I have seen it in their eyes. Forgive me, Marianna. I discussed my concern with Andrzej and your father."

"Oh?"

"Yes. I had to do what I felt was best."

"What did they say?"

"They suggested I talk with you frankly about this."

"Then speak all that is on your mind."

"Oh Marianna, I slept a full night of sleep, every night, during the week I stayed home after Christmas. Did you sleep while I was home?"

"You are right. It was difficult here."

"Antoni is still sleeping with you at night, is he not?"

"Yes, you know I keep him close during the night."

"We have talked. We have tested. We have talked some more. But, we have not used our plan to keep him warm overnight in front of the stove."

Marianna did not reply.

"I think you do not trust our plan," Helena whispered, "even though you say you do."

Marianna looked into the eyes of her dearest friend and saw tears welling up. "It is as if you can see into my heart, Helena."

"I know."

"Oh, my dear friend—you are right." Marianna stared at the basket. "I am afraid."

"That we will sleep too long?" Helena asked. "Perhaps because we are both so tired?"

"It would be terrible—if Antoni became cold and he slipped away."

Marianna lowered her head and put her hands over her face. She tried to hold in the sobs at first. But, then they erupted and woke Antoni. Helena rushed over to pick up the infant. She brought him to Marianna's lap.

"Look at him, Marianna. Do you remember when he was a lump of gray flesh, when we placed his life in God's hands?"

"Yes, I remember."

"We will find a way to ensure that Antoni does not become chilled. I promise."

Marianna tried to smile.

"Do not worry," Helena whispered. "The Lord knows we have done our part. It is time to trust again, and accept what happens."

Marianna grasped the little arms of her son and began to whisper a lullaby in Lithuanian. When she looked up, Helena was gazing at her. Marianna had expected to see some impatience. Instead, she saw a face that was filled with the pain of understanding.

"You are right, Helena. I will pray to the Blessed Mother for strength."

Bernice L. Rocque

* * *

The next day Helena walked to the woodshed and brought an armful of the new wood back to the house. She told Marianna the weight of the wood worried her. The pieces should be much lighter. One thing was certain. The windfall wood they had been burning was not going to give them the longer embers they would need overnight to keep Antoni just the right temperature in his basket. It had been so snowy and cold in January that the windfall wood was almost gone, anyway.

They all knew in their hearts that three months of seasoning was probably too little for the new wood cut down in October. Before Christmas, Nikodimas had shared his concern again about relying on the "green" wood, especially since people he knew, business people and shop owners, were saying that coal shortages were coming. He had decided that his Christmas gift to the family would be a delivery of coal. The truck arrived two days after Christmas and filled the bin in the root cellar with the shiny, small pieces of coal.

Andrzej did not argue about the generous gift from his father-in-law. He expressed to Marianna, though, how he hated the feeling of obligation to Nikodimas—yet he understood that the family could not take the chance, especially if the winter became severe. All Andrzej had asked was that Marianna and Helena try the new wood first to see if it had aged enough, before switching to coal.

So, Helena dropped three different pieces of the beautiful new wood into the fuel chamber. Three times a piece had smoked and spit, and Helena had to frantically lift it out and into a bucket. With each trial, Marianna found herself rushing into the sitting room clutching Antoni to her chest, while Helena fanned the back door, trying to coax the smoke out into the frigid air. Once the smoke dissipated, they both began to laugh. Marianna admitted to Helena that, in late December, the clatter of the coal streaming into the bin had been calming to her.

That evening after supper, Helena beckoned Nikodimas and Andrzej into the front parlor. Her news about the wood was not unexpected, but still, Andrzej sat. He agreed to switch to the coal, and then took a walk to the barn.

The family had used coal once before in one of the apartments they rented, so it took only three days for Marianna and Helena to get used to the differences required in the stove's controls. Secretly, Marianna was grateful for another reason. The small delay had helped her ready her heart for the nights ahead, when she would separate herself from her small baby.

"The coal is working well." Marianna said to her father. "Helena is happy about the change, too."

"Helena is an unusual woman to help us the way she has. I think you will be good friends for many years."

"I had forgotten how much less attention the coal fire needs."

"And fewer buckets of ash to empty," Nikodimas sang.

"Yes, I think you have mentioned that more than once, Father!"

"Well, even Andrzej should welcome less ash! Bad news is sometimes good news. I am sympathetic, though. Andrzej wanted to avoid the expense of the coal. That was why I gave it as a gift."

"Gifts can bring their own burden of obligation," Marianna remarked. "My husband and I have talked much about this since Christmas. It is fortunate that his son is more important to him than his pride."

"Andrzej is doing what he should," Nikodimas emphasized, "so that the two of you have enough money for the taxes and the loan payment."

"I see a twinkle in your eye, Father."

"Sometimes the Lord, or a concerned father, answers the prayers we do not know we will have."

"Then, let us go over the new plan so it is very clear," Marianna said with a chuckle.

"My dearest daughter, the clock chimes from the parlor will guide me, just as they have guided us all. I will sleep here on the couch in the sitting room tonight, tomorrow night, and as many nights as necessary. I want you to feel certain that Antoni is comfortable by himself in front of the stove."

"You will check him at two o'clock—and the fire? Father—perhaps you should also check him at three o'clock?"

"You can depend that I will. We will do this gradually, Marianna," Nikodimas added. "I expect that you will be anxious the first few nights and will have difficulty sleeping."

Marianna nodded and closed her eyes.

"Do not worry. There will be three of us downstairs. Each with one sleeping ear and one listening ear!"

What he had said was amusing, but she did not laugh. She wondered why her heart was pounding. She did trust him. And she trusted Helena.

That night around eight o'clock, Nikodimas bid everyone sweet dreams and settled into the worn cushions of the sitting room couch, under one of the thick down quilts Marianna had sewn in the fall. Marianna kissed Nellie and Michal good night and they started on their way upstairs with their father. Helena made herself comfortable on an extra mattress on the kitchen floor while Marianna adjusted the controls on the stove to slow the fire for the night. She fed and changed Antoni, and sat down in the wood chair.

As Marianna leaned back, she rested her hand below Antoni's warm body and drifted in light sleep. When she counted twelve chimes, Marianna got up. She checked the fire and slightly adjusted the controls. Using the eyedropper, she fed Antoni and rubbed his back gently. After changing him, she swaddled the infant in his basket, and stuck pieces of moistened cotton between the woven wood of the basket. Marianna opened the oven door and waited, then walked back and forth for several minutes before she felt the heat was gentle enough for her small infant. Sighing, she lifted and placed the basket on the table in front of the oven door, just as the half hour chimed on the clock in the parlor.

Seeing that the midwife's eyes were fully open, Marianna bowed her head slightly on her way to the wash basin. She dabbed her chest

Bernice L. Rocque

with a wet towel and dried it. After Marianna checked Antoni again, and after adjusting the pillows for her head, she sank into the cushions of the kitchen sofa and pulled the quilt up to her ears. She could not sleep at first. Thoughts streamed through her head, like waves of geese flying south.

When she heard two chimes of the clock, Marianna did not move. Soon she heard her father's heavy footsteps.

"Marianna," he whispered. "Antoni is warm. I will check him again in an hour. Do not worry. Your husband will wake you about four o'clock, before he goes outside to do his chores. Try to get sleep now."

Marianna closed her eyes and waved her forearm towards her father. She was glad he could not see her silent tears.

Chapter Ten

The winter winds blew at the house. Each evening, Nellie and Michal carried their warmed flat irons in an old woolen sock up the stairs to the metal frame bed they shared with their grandfather. On many mornings, when they greeted their mother, Michal would say the same thing.

"Matka, zimno."

"Oh, I know you are cold, Michal. Stand next to the stove and warm yourself. Rub your hands together, like this. You will soon be warm."

The large bedroom where the family slept together was directly above the kitchen stove. While Antoni slept surrounded by the gentle heat of the coals, little warmth was rising upstairs. On the coldest nights, the kitchen and the sitting room became fully occupied with sleeping bodies. Every one of the old and new down quilts was put to use.

Upon rising one morning to more snow, Nikodimas joked, "Am I home in Lithuania!"

A few neighbors continued to stop by, sometimes arriving by horse-drawn sleigh to help with shoveling and to bring food items. After most of the snowfalls, Nikodimas and Andrzej cleared the paths together. Each had spoken their gratitude for sharing the work, but Marianna could see in her husband's sullen eyes as he labored, that Andrzej's debt to her father still weighed on his mind like the snow on his shovel.

When Nikodimas learned that the Governor of Connecticut had declared a fuel emergency on the ninth of February, he mentioned it to Marianna and Helena, but not to Andrzej. Some were said to be hoarding coal. The three assumed that Andrzej had heard the same news and hoped that he had reflected more about the Christmas gift, and perhaps felt relief rather than resentment.

Following five nights of assistance from her father, Marianna had settled into a new rhythm at night without the baby on her chest. She and Antoni were getting about four hours of sleep most nights, and with Helena's help, a few good naps during the day. With her energy returning, Marianna resumed some of her household responsibilities, while Antoni spent more and more time in his basket. She knew he missed the constant contact with her body. When she heard the cry, the one that was different from his cries of hunger or discomfort, Marianna found it difficult not to pick him up, but she heeded Helena's cautions about this. "We do not want to ruin his generous nature."

Marianna had put Antoni to her breast on numerous occasions in late January. She was hopeful despite Helena's belief that he was unlikely to suckle for a while longer. The midwife had been right. One morning in mid-February, when she and Helena were laughing about something, Marianna offered the infant her breast once again. To her surprise, Antoni latched on. Helena seemed even more jubilant than Marianna. Their moments of celebration continued as Antoni kept suckling and adding ounces of weight with every week.

In the evenings, the kerosene lanterns lent a soft glow to the kitchen and the sitting

Bernice L. Rocque

room. The family would sip Marianna's coffee milk after supper and listen to the wind sing as it passed through the curved, sweeping arms of the Norway spruce. The children, usually doing their best to delay bedtime, would beg Nikodimas to play his violin. Everyone had a favorite tune, and he would happily satisfy all requests, the fingers on his left hand flying from note to note, while his right arm bowed with relish.

As much as Marianna enjoyed the evenings with Helena and the family, it was Thursday mornings she looked forward to the most. They weighed Antoni on Thursday mornings. She and Helena kept a chart, and when Andrzej returned home from work on that night, he would announce the new number at supper. Nellie and Michal would clap their hands, and after everyone had commented in one way or another, Andrzej thanked the Lord for helping his son to grow and survive another week.

Helena and Marianna experimented further with the time Marianna retired and rose. By the beginning of March, Antoni was snug in his basket by eleven o'clock. He and his mother did not rise until about four o'clock, when Andrzej started his morning chores. "Antoni is such a good baby!" Helena had expounded again and again, "the silver lining during our confinement of snow and more snow."

A warm spell spoiled them all in mid-March. Helena used the opportunity to wash many dirty clothes and bed sheets. The deep snow was mostly melted and she could hang the clothes outside to dry. Andrzej spoke to the children about not being foolhardy in this weather, so Nellie made sure that she and Michal wore heavy sweaters outside.

On the same afternoon that Antoni turned four months old, the temperature gauge rose to sixty-five degrees. After playing imaginary games outside for hours, Nellie and Michal came running into the house, the back door flying open behind them and banging, to tell their mother that they had seen a bird with a red breast. Nikodimas was close behind the children and announced with fanfare that the robins had arrived.

The moment brought joy to Marianna. The long winter was really ending. She had been feeling more like herself. How grateful she was to the Lord, to her family, and to her dear friend, Helena. Their Easter celebration that year would have added meaning.

*   *   *

On Holy Thursday morning, storm clouds were gathering when Helena started the mile hike up to the farm. A frigid cold snap, not typical for the last week of March, had surprised everyone, and was the topic of conversation in the chilly streetcar.

By the time Helena was halfway up the street, the ten-degree wind felt like icicles stabbing her face. On the final stretch of road near the house, a snow quall pounded her, making it difficult to see. With the outstretched limbs of the Norway spruce guiding the way, Helena made it to the front porch. She walked through the door with a big smile, her frozen hands holding a tall sweet Easter bread filled with plump raisins.

Marianna hung Helena's wet outer clothes to dry and wrapped an afghan around her friend. Then, she dragged two chairs right up to the stove, so that Helena could warm herself while they talked.

The two were well into a second slice with more coffee, when Helena stood up and walked across the kitchen to the south window, drawn by a flicker of light. Marianna followed, her curiosity aroused. The squall had ended and giant snowflakes were floating to the ground, becoming transparent and sparkling each time rays of sunlight flashed through the thinning cloud cover.

"Look Marianna, over there."

Helena pointed to a flock of robins pecking through the inch of snow that had accumulated. Marianna leaned into the sitting room. With her forefinger against her lips, Marianna beckoned Nellie and Michal to come quietly to the kitchen window.

"It is the family of robins!" Nellie whispered. "The snow will not hurt them, will it, Matka?"

"They will be fine," Marianna said. "Do not worry."

She cradled her Antosh in his satchel, noticing a wisp of a smile from him before he nestled against her body—all five pounds of him. Marianna smiled to herself. *Here on the farm, the land is generous with food and life.*

"These determined robins look very healthy!" Helena remarked.

Marianna looked up. Helena's eyes were reflecting the light from the outside. This wonderful friend was like the sister she never had. So many times, one knew the other's thoughts. A wide grin appeared on each of their faces, and then the two recited the words of Marianna's favorite poem.

"It is not spring...
until the robin walks on snow."

About the Author

Bernice L. Rocque is an educator, family historian, writer, and avid gardener. She grew up in Norwich, Connecticut in the surroundings described in her novella, *Until the Robin Walks on Snow*. She has authored numerous business articles associated with her work in libraries, training and development, and project management. Articles she has written about her family have appeared in the *Norwich Bulletin*, *Good Old Days* magazine, and *Family Chronicle*. Ms. Rocque lives in Trumbull, Connecticut with her husband and two cats.

Wedding of Helena and Mike.
Norwich, Connecticut, 1913.

Author's Notes

INTRODUCTION

The purpose of these notes is to identify elements of the story that are fact, or garnered through accounts of family history, or based on research, and to provide further background on some of them. The section was intended for my family, but other readers may find the notes of interest.

The last section, the List of Sources Consulted, provides citations for sources used to research and verify information. That section also offers internet links to a portion of the research materials.

Though the story is written in English, the characters would have been speaking Polish to each other, unless otherwise noted. When America is mentioned, either in the story or in these notes, the reference is to the United States.

The physical descriptions of the characters are based on photographs, documents, and personal recollections. The characterizations were developed from my own memories and impressions, as well as those shared by relatives and friends of the family.

With one exception discussed in the final author's note, the weather descriptions were based on the weather recorded or forecasted for the Norwich area, Connecticut, or tri-state region (CT, MA, NY).

For purposes of reference, Michal, the 2-year-old child in the story, was my father. Marianna was my grandmother and Andrzej my grandfather. Nikodimas was my great-grandfather. I never met him, but I collected (and continue to collect) many stories about him from his grandchildren and others who knew him. I was acquainted with Helena and members of the Bychkowsky family.

The pronunciation of character names and Polish words used in the story follows.

Marianna --- Mahr-ee-ahn-a (last syllable barely pronounced)

Helena --- El-lay-nya (silent "H" and first "e" soft)

Andrzej --- Ahn-jee

Nikodimas --- Nik-caw-dim-yuss

Michal --- Mee-hal

Antosh --- Ahn-toosh

Jan --- Yahn

Mikolaj ---Meek-o-why

The pronunciation and meaning of most of the Polish words that appear in the story follows.

Matka --- Mott-ka --- Mother

Tata --- Tah-tah ---Daddy

Dziadzia --- Jah-jah --- Grampa

Dziekuje --- Jen-koo-ya --- Thank you

Na zdrowie --- Nahz-drove-ya --- To your health!

Pierogi --- peer-o-gey --- Filled dumpling(s)

Zimno --- zimm-noe --- Cold

In 1922, the view out the east window (from a sitting position) would have been of the trees at the edge of the forest, as described in the story. The view is similar today, except that there is an additional shed in the foreground, built a few years after this story takes place. Today, it is the only surviving building on the property from that time, aside from the house. In the 1922 kitchen, the sofa was in front of the east wall's window, as described. The stove was located on the north wall of the kitchen, kitty-corner to the sofa. The back door was on the south wall, kitty-corner to the other end of the sofa. The west wall, which adjoined the sitting room, had free standing metal cabinets and other storage. It is likely that Marianna moved her chair as needed to surround herself with comfortable heat from the stove.

My cousin, Don, supplied the information that our grandmother, Marianna, used the skin-to-skin approach to keep Antoni warm. She told Don that she sat for "a long time" with the infant on her chest. He said that she didn't give a period of time, but he guessed by the way she emphasized the words and rolled her eyes with a smile that the duration was probably a few months. Don learned about this in a conversation with our grandmother later in her life.

The skin-to-skin approach has been familiar for probably hundreds of years to some people, but it does not appear to be universally known or used. Even today, in third world nations, hypothermia is a leading cause of infant mortality, as pointed out by V. Kumar et al. (See my List of Sources Consulted.)

There is an interesting skin-to-skin use case documented by the late Jennifer Worth in her memoir of delivering babies in the neighborhoods of London's East End during the 1950s. The mother, Conchita Warren, a war bride from Spain, bore her 25th child early, after falling just outside her home. The child was thought to be barely at six months gestation and weighed about a pound and a half, similar to Antoni. The mother would not allow the medical team who delivered the baby at her home to take him to the hospital. Instead, she placed the baby between her breasts and fed him using a fine glass rod that her daughter used for decorating cakes. Jennifer Worth's midwife trilogy of books has served as the basis of a 2012 BBC television series.

Incubators and modern medical techniques, refined over the last century (and especially the last forty years), have greatly decreased the mortality rates of premature babies. In the last few decades, interest in the skin-to-skin technique has increased. Research on the technique has shown that it can be extremely beneficial for all babies, including premature infants who do not have serious physical challenges, aside from birth weight. According to V. Kumar et al., researchers of neonatal hypothermia in developing countries, the main benefit of the skin-to-skin approach is optimal warming of the child by the mother's body. As compared to artificial warming methods, the technique also brings more rapid physiological stability to the baby's major bodily functions, builds a strong bond between mother and child, and speeds the ability of the baby to feed. Today, use of the skin-to-skin approach appears to be on the increase. Some call it the kangaroo technique.

A father and son team who rebuild antique wood stoves (Antique Stove Hospital in Rhode Island) and served as a resource for me said that they have heard scores of stories over the years about parents in the general time period of the antique stoves they rebuild who used the heat of wood stoves to keep babies warm and also to try to save premature infants. Stories are common from the time period of this book about premature infants placed in shoeboxes near the heat of the stove with everything from minimal to attentive care.

A story appeared in the <u>Bangor Daily News</u> on April 28, 2012, celebrating the 100th birthday of a woman being honored for the extraordinary lifetime contributions she had made. She was born weighing a pound and a half, just like Antoni. The doctor, in her case, did not expect her to live more than a day. He advised her parents to put her in a shoebox and then told them, "It could serve as a cradle and a coffin."

CHAPTER ONE

Antoni's birth occurred November 23, 1922, according to the Office of the City Clerk, Norwich, Connecticut. His birth was registered on December 1, 1922. He was the fifth child born to Mary, of which three children were living.

According to the records in the Office of the City Clerk, the first child of Marianna and Andrzej, named Anthony, was born October 29, 1916 and died within thirty minutes of his birth. The family history is that the second child was stillborn. There do not appear to be civil or church records for that child. The third child, Nellie, was born July 21, 1918 and Michael, the fourth child, was born September 29, 1920.

Nellie's birth record indicates that she was initially named Paulina. That name was struck on the record and Nellie inserted. Both Nellie and the name Angela appear on Nellie's baptismal record at St. Joseph's Church. The Polish name for Nellie is Aniela and for Angelina is Anielcia. In the letter from Lithuania at a later date, Nellie is referred to as Aniele.

According to family history, Antoni was weighed on the butter scale.

The story about Andrzej reviving his niece, Anna, was told to me in the late 1970s by the niece he saved. At the time, Ann Kuzmich Onuparik was helping me to research the family history. According

Bernice L. Rocque

to Ann's daughter, Marilyn, her mother was born October 14, 1910.

In the late 1970s, Ann Onuparik worked with a friend who knew how to read the "old" Russian to translate an internal pass that my grandfather, Andrzej, had retained. Andrzej would have used the document when traveling inside Russian-occupied Poland. That document indicates that he reported in February 1911, as required, and was associated with the 1906 Russian Army Second Reserve. The document indicated he would have to report again in one year. He chose to leave Europe within the month. Andrzej arrived in the United States in March 1911.

Andrzej boarded with his sister, Natalia, and her husband, John Kuzmich. Natalie, as she was known, arrived in America in May 1904.

According to my father, Marianna (his mother) was the only surviving child of Nikodimas and Paulina (Damusis) Borovkis at the time her father brought Marianna to America in July 1914. Marianna's six brothers did not reach adulthood.

According to the 1922 street directory for Norwich, Connecticut, less than half of the residents on the street where the family lived had telephones.

CHAPTER TWO

Helena wonders why this tiny infant is not struggling to breathe. The likely reason is that the surfactant in Antoni's lungs probably developed earlier than usual. Less than one percent of extremely premature babies are born with surfactant. Without it, the lungs get stuck and cannot stay open, eventually collapsing. Surfactant, a critically needed substance that coats and lubricates the cells of the lungs, makes the lung tissue more elastic.

A newborn with Respiratory Distress Syndrome (RDS) is likely deficient in surfactant. In 1922, infants with RDS typically would gasp until they died. Imagine the heartbreak for a parent watching this happen. Today, respirators are used and surfactant introduced to remedy the deficiency, thereby saving many infants. For a summary of Respiratory Distress Syndrome see my List of Sources Consulted (U.S. Heart and Lung Institute).

In Marianna's case, as Helena suggests in the story, the reason for the surfactant developing early in Antoni's lungs might have been that Marianna's body was under a lot of stress due to the recent move of the family to the farm property and all the work that needed to be done to prepare them for the winter. The current medical belief is that the mother's body may, in some situations, be anticipating that the baby could be born early, and it accelerates the development of the baby's critical systems.

Eastern European cultures of this time expected the women to contribute in major ways to the household, including earning income. Studies of infant mortality during the time of Antoni's birth found that babies of Eastern European families had a higher mortality rate than many other ethnic groups.

Anthony, the first child of Marianna and Andrzej, died thirty minutes following the birth. The record in the Office of the City Clerk, Norwich, CT served as both a birth and death record. The stated primary cause of death was "premature birth" and the contributing cause of death was "inanition," or exhaustion. At the time of his birth in 1916, the parents resided at 134 Yantic Street in Norwich along with five other families. Undertakers Shea & Burke handled the burial of Anthony in St. Mary's Cemetery, in Norwich, in the special section there for babies and small children. The location of this special section is in the upper far left corner of the cemetery, as you face it from the street. His grave is unmarked, as are many in this area of the cemetery.

There is no family history information that Antoni, the baby in this story, had trouble breathing, feeding, digesting food, or passing waste. So, though some readers may have expected a story line that dealt with one or more of these challenges, I opted not to fictionalize physical challenges that he did not appear to have had.

The elevation of Norwich ranges from about 50 feet near the Thames River in downtown Norwich to near 500 feet. The farm property, purchased in 1922, is located approximately 360 feet above sea level and about five miles from downtown Norwich.

We don't know who alerted our family to the property for sale on Bean Hill, but it could have been a relative or friend. The older historic core of

Bean Hill was listed as the Bean Hill Historic District, in the National Register of Historic Places application in 1982. (See U.S. Department of the Interior in the List of Sources Consulted.) However, in the early 1900s the area referred to as Bean Hill by residents extended further into the streets emanating from the green on West Town Street.

There were woolen mills located in Yantic and on Sturtevant Street (off West Town Street). Palmer Brothers quilt mill, where Marianna worked in the 1930s, was located in Fitchville, not far from Yantic.

In 1920, the population of Norwich was approximately 30,000. Norwich was a destination of choice for many waves of immigrants. By the early 1900s it offered a diversified industrial and manufacturing base with reasonable job prospects for both skilled and unskilled workers. The town also provided downtown city water and sewage systems, accessible local travel on electrified streetcars, a free public library, well regarded schools, numerous churches and synagogues, and reasonable housing of higher quality and comfort than the immigrant ghettoes of larger cities, such as New York and Chicago.

About forty percent of the farm property's acreage was cleared land that could be used for crops and/or pastures. The remaining land, spanning the rear half of the property, was gently sloping woods.

Marianna loved flowers, especially irises. When I was a child in the 1950s, my grandmother grew more than 25 varieties of iris. In early June, she would cut a gigantic bouquet for me to bring to my wonderful teacher at Samuel Huntington School. I think the bouquets went to Mrs. Richardson, Mrs. Sullivan, Mrs. Kennedy, and Mrs. Parkhurst in different years. The irises were magnificently colored and had an unforgettably beautiful scent. My grandmother grew all the flowers mentioned in the story and many others. She also brewed special teas and developed natural remedies from the many herbs she grew, as well as from plants, like thistle, that grew wild in the fields or woods.

In general, immigrants in the early 1900s found the wages in America far greater than what they earned in Europe, and jobs were generally easier to find here. Ordinary expenses in America were not onerous in many cities and towns, such as Norwich, so immigrants were able to save.

Bernice L. Rocque

The purchase price of the farm was recorded as "one dollar and other considerations." This custom, apparent in many real estate transactions of this time, lent some air of privacy regarding the actual price. The $1,000 promissory note mentioned in the story is also contained in the records, along with a release stamp. With the help of the staff in the Norwich Office of the City Clerk, we established the likely purchase price of the farm as about $2,200, using the tax stamps affixed to the property transfer record. The Norwich Bulletin printed all the property assessments for Norwich, by owner name, in their January 29, 1923 newspaper edition. Andrzej's property was assessed at less than $1,000, possibly $839. The number is not legible on the microfilm.

According to my father (Michal), the obligation of the $1,000 loan did weigh on my grandfather's mind. Andrzej talked about it often, so much so that this, and the Great Depression, must have influenced my father's thinking on this subject. My father avoided loans his entire life. He never took on a house mortgage, car loans, or credit cards. He thought long and hard before he signed a $1,000 loan for me for my freshman year of college.

The referenced portrait appears in Chapter One of this book. The studio of Peter Antoofian, a well-known photographer in Norwich at the time, also produced the wedding photograph of Helena and Mike, which appears at the start of this section.

My Aunt Vee shared the story about my grandmother refusing to take up residence in the roach-infested farmhouse until it was fumigated.

Lye soap was a commonly used cleaner in this time. My 80-something relatives tell me it is the likely product used to clean the farmhouse.

The gray shed was located about twenty-five feet from the northeast corner of the house, to the right of a small woodshed. This gray shed was used for activities connected to preserving the meat of freshly slaughtered animals. By the mid-1920s, the adjacent new red shed had a portion dedicated to meat preparation.

According to family history, at the time Marianna's brothers attended school, Prussian Germany was located across the Nemanus River, not far from where the Borovskis family lived. Out of necessity, Marianna and her father spoke German, in addition

Bernice L. Rocque

to Lithuanian, Polish, and Russian. Marianna did not attend the same school as her brothers. Instead, she attended a school that taught the domestic arts, as was typical for girls at that time. Her father, Nikodimas, schooled her at home in many of the subjects her brothers were learning. He taught her using mostly "black market" books, which had to be replaced often, according to family history. When Russian patrols were near, the books were tossed into the fire.

Marianna loved crocheting, detested sewing, and picked mushrooms. She saved and reused the flour sacks in many different ways, including sewing underpants for the children during their school years. All of the nut varieties were collected by this family and also subsequent generations of the family. I can recall picking up all of these types of nuts in a paper bag and cracking them on the front steps at my house when I was a child. It takes a little practice, but it is possible to crack the shell of a fragile shagbark nut without smashing the plump nut inside. The shagbarks were the favorite of my father. In the fall, he would take my sisters and me nutting, and sometimes our cousins would join us. The hazelnuts were about one-quarter the size of those we buy today in the supermarket, but the taste is similar.

Most mothers returned to their responsibilities within ten days of giving birth, according to U.S. government reports of the time.

CHAPTER THREE

The Nemanus River is one of the largest in Europe. It winds its way through Lithuania. Marianna and Nikodimas were from Grinaiciai, a town located in southwestern Lithuania on the south bank of the river. Grinaiciai is located about sixty miles west of Kaunas and a few miles from Sudargas. Archeological evidence of fortifications in Sudargas and Grinaiciai suggest they were fortresses in the middle ages.

When they were children, Marianna and her brother Antanas were very close. In her photograph albums, Aunt Vee has black and white photos of a wake and funeral in which a young boy is resting in the casket. The photos are not labeled, but my great grandmother, Paulina, appears to be in the photos.

Bernice L. Rocque

We believe the photos may be of Marianna's deceased brother, Antanas.

According to Ellis Island records, "Marianna Birowska" arrived July 6, 1914 from Rotterdam aboard the Nieuw Amsterdam. The ship was built in 1906. It had one funnel and four masts; it was the last major liner to be fitted with auxiliary sails. Its passenger capacity was 2,886. The manifest recorded the information that she had blue eyes and was born in Resgalun. This is probably the current town of Rezgaliai, located near their residence of Grinaiciai and not far from Sudargas.

In a conversation many years after Uncle Tony and Aunt Albina were married, Marianna and Aunt Albina's mother, Victoria, discovered that the two of them came to America on the same voyage, though they did not know each other at the time.

The family history is that Nikodimas accompanied his daughter, Marianna, to America. According to the Ellis Island records, Nikodimas does not appear on the same list of passengers. However, when asked, Marianna indicates she is going to her father's, and gives his name. We think he used either someone else's passport, which was common, or arranged for an alternate passport. By 1914, he had traveled back and forth to America enough times to know the practices at Ellis Island, as well as benefit by what family members and friends reported.

The family history is that Marianna and Andrzej lived next door to Helena and Mike on High Street before moving to the farm. The Norwich street directory for 1922 does list the two men at 27 and 25 High Street, thus verifying the information that they lived "next door" to each other. Numerous Polish families lived on High Street and on neighboring streets in the Thamesville area of town. High Street overlooked the Thames River, and was one of the streets located between West Main and West Thames Streets. The houses on High Street no longer exist. They were torn down at one stage of redevelopment in the city.

In the List of Sources Consulted, there is a link to a web site about Norwich neighborhoods. That internet article contains a post card of Norwich, circa 1907, that appears to be a view of High Street and the Thames River from the higher elevation of Mount Pleasant Street.

Helena's birth date is not consistent in various vital and church records. It appears that she was born December 1 in either 1891 or 1892, so she would have been about 31 years of age at the time of this story. We believe it was Helena who registered the birth on December 1. In the story, she reports the birth on her way home. My uncle told me that birthdays were not celebrated in the time period of the story to the same degree we celebrate them today. It is possible that Helena returned home that particular day because it was her birthday, but the more likely reasons are the responsibility of reporting the birth in a timely manner and the urgency of scheduling Antoni's baptism. Of course, considering how efficient Helena was, all three reasons may have influenced the choice of the date!

The Seth Thomas clock usually sat on a shelf of the wood hutch, located just inside the sitting room from the kitchen. It was a gift from Marianna's father and she did treasure it.

CHAPTER FOUR

During family history interviews I conducted in the 1960s and 1970s, my Aunt Nellie shared the story about how her father used the edge of a wet spoon to release water droplets onto Antoni's mouth.

The tale about the three brothers is fairly well known to those with Eastern European origins. A simple search on the Internet can surface many different versions of the story. I chose to weave some of their common elements into this version, while also embedding some historical and philosophical points that Nikodimas might have shared. According to Wittke (see my List of Sources Consulted), one of the triggers for immigration to the U.S. in the early 20th century was that "Polish villages suffered acutely from overpopulation because of primitive agricultural methods."

The final scene of this chapter in which the children get a "nice squirt or two of milk" is based on the childhood experiences of my Uncle Tony.

CHAPTER FIVE

Fitchville is a small town located a few miles northwest of Bean Hill. According to the 1920 U.S. Census, the Bychkowskys lived there.

At the time of this story, the actual date of Thanksgiving was announced each year in the United States. In 1922, President Warren G. Harding declared, via Presidential proclamation, that Thanksgiving would be celebrated on the 30th of November. My Uncle Tony told me that the family did not celebrate this American holiday, typically, when he and his siblings were children.

Coffee milk was a beverage mixed by my grandmother, Marianna, using mostly rich milk and a little coffee, probably left over from the breakfast pot. She would leave the coffee milk on the "cooler" side of the stove, with just enough heat to stay warm for several hours. Learning about the coffee milk during the interviews for this story was a revelation for me. For years, I had watched my father order coffee at restaurants with all sorts of instructions to the waitress (various combinations of coffee, extra milk, and/or water) because he always found restaurant coffee too strong. At home, my mother made coffee so weak that my relatives called it "dish water." Now I know my father was searching all those years for the taste of that coffee milk from his childhood.

The feast of St. Michael, the Archangel, is September 29, my father's birthday. It was common in this time to name children after a saint if they were born on or near that saint's feast day. The other most typical way a child was named was after a family member, alive or deceased. In my father's case, it is interesting that he grew up to be a protective sort of person, possibly due to priming by his parents, grandfather, and godmother, Helena.

Mikolaj Bychkowsky was related to my grandfather, somehow through Andrzej's mother, Anastasia Bychkowsky. In any gathering of family and friends, Mikolaj Bychkowsky was noticeably the tallest person in the room. My uncle told me that Mikolaj was a wise and respected person and that he was very nice to his wife, Savetta. My Aunt Vee told me that Sally was smart in school and particularly good in math. She had an older sister, Sophie.

According to a commemorative booklet about the history of the St. Nicholas Russian Orthodox Church in Norwich, Mikolaj was elected as an officer of the church's first Parish Council in January 1915. Construction of the new church began after Easter that year and the church opened near the end of 1915. Mikolaj Bychkowsky is listed as the "collector" for the Fitchville area in 1915, along with a relative of his, Antip Pershaec. Andrzej's sister, Natalia Kuzmich, was also a member of this church.

Ann Onuparik, the daughter of Natalia, mentioned in the notes for Chapter One, belonged to the Russian Orthodox Church. She made me aware that when she and her parents were growing up, it was traditional that, if the parents were communicants of different churches, then the male children were brought up in the church of the father and the female children in the church of the mother. Since Andrzej's father, John, was Polish and attended the Catholic Church, so did Andrzej. His sister, Natalia, was brought up attending the Russian Orthodox Church, the church of their mother, Anastasia.

My Aunt Vee told me that her mother, Marianna, was quite skilled at running the stove and preferred to be the only one managing the controls.

The instances in the story of Andrzej making fun of Marianna for one thing or another are fictional examples, but this was characteristic of their relationship during their marriage, as described by all their children.

The age information of the previous owner of the property was drawn from the 1920 U.S. Census.

The baskets that my grandfather, Andrzej, wove were distinctive in their pattern. Baskets very similar to the ones I remember are still made today in Belarus. My grandfather originated from an area of Poland that is part of Belarus today. His town of origin is still in question. But, based on a variety of documents, I believe he lived in the district of Bakshty, in the southern part of Ashmyany province, in the gubernia of Vilna. (These were the Russian political districts at the time he left Europe.)

When my cousins and I were children, my grandmother (Marianna) kept her little chicks warm each spring using the barely heated oven of her wood stove. The oven door would be open, extended straight out. My cousin, Coni, and I remember that the chicks would sometimes jump down from the oven and run around the kitchen floor. Our grandmother would laugh, bend over and scoop them up, and place them back in the oven.

CHAPTER SIX

The birth certificate for Antoni indicates registration of his birth on December 1, 1922. From the Franklin Street trolley line, it would have been a short walk up either Bath or Willow Street to the town hall in downtown Norwich.

Helena was also the midwife and godmother for Michal, Antoni's older brother.

The feast of the Immaculate Conception is celebrated on December 8th. The baptism took place on December 3rd.

Family history is the source of the story references about Nikodimas trying to convince Paulina to come to America, the houses in Lithuania, and the accidental drowning of two of Marianna's brothers while swimming in the Nemanus River.

Both family history and Ellis Island records indicate that Nikodimas had traveled to America more than once. According to one Ellis Island record, Nikodimas traveled to New York in 1911 (aboard the Nieuw Amsterdam, the same ship that he and my grandmother used in 1914). Nikodimas named a brother-in-law living in Brooklyn as his contact. He also answered "yes" that he had been in America previously, and to the question of where, he responded "Norwich." My father told me that Nikodimas had traveled as far west as the wheat fields in Kansas.

According to family history, Jan Sak's wife, Anna, returned to Poland early in their marriage. In the Norwich vital records, there is no trace of her after their marriage on October 10, 1911. Yet, she was still listed as his wife on his death certificate. Apparently, returning to the old country was not uncommon, though the return could cause resentment in a family who paid for the cost of passage, which was a considerable sum for many at that time. In some cases, the individual came to America for the purpose of employment and sending dollars to their family back in Europe. This was true for Anna, a female relative of Helena. Anna's mother and sister in Poland depended upon the money she sent home to them, according to Anna's granddaughter.

According to family history, Nikodimas brought Marianna to America in July 1914, shortly before the outbreak of World War I. He did not travel back to Lithuania until the war ended. His specialty was metalwork, though my father always said that his grandfather was a highly skilled carpenter as well. Nikodimas worked as a supervisor in the Hopkins & Allen gun factory in downtown Norwich during WWI. They did give him a shotgun and a violin when he left.

The "green" mentioned near the end of this chapter is sometimes called the Huntington Green. It is part of the Bean Hill Historic District.

CHAPTER SEVEN

Jan Sak, born about 1892, is still described by our family (and friends of our family) as a person that everyone liked. According to the late husband of a family friend, "everyone knew Jan Sak—and Jan Sak knew everyone." In my grandparents' group of friends, he was one of the first to buy a car. Even today, people who knew him or of him, recall how he graciously carted people around town, across Connecticut, and even to other states on occasion. He is listed as the godfather of numerous children, and by all accounts was a dapper dresser, always had a kind word, and was a truly beloved figure.

He was employed as a weaver at the Ponemah Mill and for J.B. Martin, which produced high quality velvet fabric.

According to family history, a Dr. Thompson came out to verify the birth soon after the birth was registered. According to my Uncle Tony, the doctor had practiced for decades and contributed the comments as told in the story. I believe this doctor was George Thompson, MD, a prominent citizen of Norwich, who in 1922 would have been about sixty years of age and would have practiced medicine for more than thirty years. By 1922, he had already been the town's health officer for fifteen years. (See Marshall, in my List of Sources Consulted, for a brief biography of him.)

A chart attributed to Pfaundler, a well known pediatrician, appeared in a 1917 article by Alan Brown (see List of Sources Consulted). In the chart, Pfaundler provides the likelihood of mortality in the first few weeks of life for various premature birth weights and gestational ages. The lowest weight he lists is 2 pounds 3 ounces. For that weight, the likely mortality rate listed is 95 percent. At three pounds, the mortality rate is listed as 65 percent.

According to the U.S. Department of the Census, the infant mortality rate for 1922 was 76 deaths per 1000 births, or about 1 death per 14 births. One third of those deaths occurred in the first seven days of infancy. The projected U.S. infant mortality rate for 2012 is about 6 deaths per 1000 births, according to the CIA World Factbook and other reputable sources. There are a number of countries with a projected 2012 rate lower than the United States.

My cousin, Don, also shared with me that our grandmother told him that she felt that if Antoni could hear her heart beating, he would feel safe and stay with them.

When I was growing up, my grandmother was a very busy person. I would often see her doing one thing with one hand and another thing with the other hand. In those situations, she had a distinctive way of using her thumb and forefinger to spread something open so that she could see inside or to grab something she needed.

In Lithuania, singing is still a national pastime. Numerous song festivals occur there each year.

My Aunt Vee told me that my grandmother, Marianna, loved reading poems because they were like songs to her. She clipped many from a Lithuanian newspaper she received.

Both Nikodimas and Andrzej valued education. The family history is that Andrzej's father, John, was a teacher in Poland. We believe he taught the elementary grades and probably all subjects. Like Nikodimas, Andrzej sometimes told stories to his children, often fairy tales, such as Grimm. He also helped his children and their cousins with math homework.

According to the records at St. Joseph's Church, Antoni's baptism occurred on Sunday, December 3, 1922. Father P. Stroka performed the baptism.

When I first began to write this story, I expected to learn that a priest had come to the farm to baptize Antoni, given his fragile condition. But, my aunt and uncle insisted that would not have happened, though a priest would have driven out to bless bread. Antoni's baptismal record does not reflect any special circumstances.

The reason his parents probably took Antoni to be baptized so soon after his birth was that they feared if he died prior to receiving the sacrament, he might spend eternity in limbo. Until quite recently, the afterlife fate of an infant that died before being baptized had not been as clear as many Catholics would have liked, leading to considerable apprehension over the centuries by parents whose infants expired not long after birth. From 2005-2007, an International Theological Commission, appointed by the Pope, reexamined this issue. The Commission reiterated the long standing guidance of the Church that newborns should be baptized as soon as reasonably possible, but that "there are theological and liturgical reasons to hope that infants who die without baptism may be saved and brought into eternal happiness, even if there is not an explicit teaching on this question found in Revelation." (See my List of Sources Consulted under International Theological Commission.)

CHAPTER EIGHT

Christmas Eve, called Wigilia in Polish, was a more important holiday than Christmas Day to my relatives during their lives. However, the children waited with anticipation for the arrival of Santa who would usually bring them modest gifts on Christmas Day, such as oranges, bananas, and handmade scarves, mittens, and socks.

Uncle Tony said that sometimes they cut the tree and other times they dug it out and later transplanted it. In the early years at the farm, it was often placed in a bucket with sand and water.

Our family's Wigilia celebrations relaxed somewhat over the years, with some traditions being shed as the family became more Americanized. The traditions that were still going strong by the 1950s and 1960s were the sharing of the wafer, the white tablecloth, the brandy toast upon arrival, and the twelve dishes, including smelts.

The shot glasses with the tiny glass handles, used for the Wigilia toast, were housed in the curved, glass front hutch in the parlor.

It was common for Catholic adults to fast on important holy days and for Polish people to visit with their relatives on Christmas Day.

Kucia --- pronounced kash-a. This was the fermented cereal that the children did not like. My aunt and uncle tell me that it was usually left for Santa, as part of the little offerings.

Krustai --- pronounced kroos-ty. This dessert was served on Christmas Eve and on other holidays. It was made by dropping strips of sweet dough into hot oil for just a short while, until golden brown. The dough skin bubbled and would gently twist like ribbons. Before serving, the pieces received a light dusting of confectionary sugar.

Kolachki --- pronounced kloch-key.

In taste, thickness, and texture, the wafer is much like the host served at communion during a Catholic Mass. The main difference is that the Christmas Eve wafer was one large piece rather than small circular pieces that had been cut for individual servings.

The Christmas Eve custom about being ready to receive unexpected visitors was actually practiced all year long. My father told me that Polish and Lithuanian people in this time, (and perhaps now still) were hospitable to unannounced visitors every day of the year, even when they did not have much food to share.

Lithuanian and Polish people share many of the same Christmas Eve customs. Please see the List of Sources Consulted for some of the wonderful Internet sites that describe their celebrations of Christmas Eve.

Years ago, an uncle of mine on my mother's side of the family told me about the unreliability of tires in the 1920s and 1930s. He said it was not unusual to replace a tire on trips of only a few hours, sometimes less.

The ending of the dinner due to concern about germs is fictional, but my uncle and aunt cannot recall ever seeing Mike Lebicz at the farm in the years after Antoni was born, though both Helena and Jan Sak visited frequently, as did many other people. Our working theory is that there were hard feelings by Mike about something in the years around this story. We just don't know what. So, I elected to write a fictional reason that will explain his absence from the farm in the stories to come, while highlighting how terrified and protective Marianna might have become (especially after living through the 1918 flu epidemic four years earlier) if someone came into the house with a contagious condition while this infant was so vulnerable.

CHAPTER NINE

Caraway seeds can relieve nausea and dizziness.

Peter Labenski told me that when he was a boy, he would go often with his father to visit Helena on High Street. He said that his father, the founder of the Labenski Funeral Home, once remarked that Helena could get more meals out of one chicken than anyone he knew.

CHAPTER TEN

My father (Michal) told me many years ago that his earliest memory was of being cold at night in the wintertime. I had asked him if it was typical to feel cold at night during the winter months when he was a child. He said that unless a fierce wind was blowing on a very cold night they were usually comfortable sleeping. They used their heated irons (like miniature flat irons of today, but solid iron) to keep their feet warm and snuggled under the generously stuffed down quilts. My father believed that the winter he felt so cold sleeping was the winter when his younger brother was born and his mother used a slow fire in the stove at night to keep the heat output just right for the new baby.

According to the *Norwich Bulletin,* Governor Templeton declared a fuel emergency in Connecticut on February 9, 1923.

Much of this story is based on fact, family history and/or research. I have fictionalized it and written the story "that might have happened." As far as I know, the snow squall that concludes the story is fiction, unlike the other descriptions of the weather which are based on historical weather data. While driving, I have experienced two severe snow squalls in Connecticut, both around April 1. They started suddenly, like squalls do, became very intense, and were over relatively quickly, even though it seemed an eternity of anxiety. I felt the squall was a fitting metaphor to pair with the robins.

There was a real poem containing the final words of the story. It was Marianna's favorite, according to my Uncle Tony, her Antosh.

Bernice L. Rocque

List of Sources Consulted

Alexander, June Granatir. Daily Life in Immigrant America, 1870-1920. Ivan R. Dee, Publisher, 2007.

Allen Frederick Lewis. Only Yesterday. Harper & Row, 1964.

Ancestry.com.

Antique Stove Hospital. Available at: http://stovehospital.com/

Balzekas Museum of Lithuanian Culture, Chicago, IL.

Bean Hill Historic District. Living Places. The Gombach Group, Copyright 1997-2012. Available at: http://www.livingplaces.com/CT/New_London_Cou nty/Norwich_City/Bean_Hill_Historic_District.html

Brown, Alan, M.B. and George Ruggles, B.S., M.B. The Care and Feeding of the Premature Infant. Archives of Pediatrics, Vol. 34, 1917, pp. 609-616. Available at: http://www.neonatology.org/classics/brown2.html

Collins, Selwyn D., PH.D. *The Influenza Epidemic of 1928-29 with Comparative Data for 1918-1919.* American Journal of Public Health and THE NATION'S HEALTH, Vol. XII, No. 2, February 1930. Available at: www.ncbi.nlm.gov/pmc/articles

Courter, Gay. The Midwife. Houghton Mifflin, 1981.

Courter, Gay. The Midwife's Advice. Penguin Books, 1992.

Davies, Norman. God's Playground: A History of Poland. Columbia University Press, 1982.

Davis, Marie, R.N. The Premature Infant. 2006. Available at: http://www.lactationconsultant.info/preterm.html

Durham, Roger, M.D. *Notes on the Care of Premature Infants.* Archives of Pediatrics, Vol. 29, 1912, pp. 438-441. Available at: http://www.neonatology.org/classics/durham.html

Encyclopedia Lituanica. Boston, MA, 1976.

Familysearch.org.

Harrison, Judy. *Honoring Incredible Dedication: Husson celebrates 100th birthday of woman who*

wasn't expected to live a day. <u>Bangor Daily News</u>,
April 28, 2012.

Hendrick, Burton J. *Solving the Problem of Infant
Mortality.* <u>Harper's Magazine</u>, October 1917, pp.
723-729. Available at:
<u>http://www.neonatology.org/classics/hendrick.htm
l</u>

International Theological Commission. <u>The Hope of
Salvation for Infants Who Die Without Being
Baptised</u>. Vatican, 2007. Available at:
<u>http://www.vatican.va/roman_curia/congregations
/cfaith/cti_documents/rc_con_cfaith_doc_2007041
9_un-baptised-infants_en.html</u>

Kudirka, Juozas. *Christmas Eve.* <u>The Lithuanians</u>,
Lithuanian Folk Culture, 1991. Available at:
<u>http://thelithuanians.com/bookthelithuanians/no
de17.html#section0017</u>

Kumar, V., J.C. Shearer, A. Kumar, and G.L.
Darmstadt. *STATE OF THE ART. Neonatal
Hypothermia in Low Resource Settings: A Review.*
<u>Journal of Perinatology</u>, 2009, pp. 1-12.

Laskas, Gretchen Moran. <u>The Midwife's Tale</u>. Dial
Press, 2003.

Lithuanian American Community, Inc. *Lithuanian Customs and Traditions: Christmas Eve.* Available at: http://javlb.org/educat/tradicijos/kucios.html

Lithuanian American Community, Inc. Arizona Chapter. *Lithuanian Christmas Traditions.* Available at: http://www.lithaz.org/arts/xmas.html

Lau, Rosalind G.L. Stress Experiences of Parents with Premature Infants in a Special Care Nursery. Victoria University, Doctoral Thesis, 2001.

Makin, Amanda. *Breastfeeding My Premature Baby.* New Beginnings, Vol. 25, No. 3, 2008, pp. 10-11. Available at: http://www.llli.org/nb/nbmayjun08p10.html

Marshall, Benjamin Tinkham, ed. A Modern History of New London County Connecticut. Lewis Historical Publishing Company, 1922.

National Oceanic and Atmospheric Administration. *Boston Seasonal Snowfall Statistics (1920-1996).* Available at: http://www.erh.noaa.gov/box/climate/snowbos.html

National Oceanic and Atmospheric Administration, National Climatic Data Center. *Connecticut Precipitation September 1895 - August 2012.*

Available at: http://www.ncdc.noaa.gov/temp-and-precip/time-series/index.php?parameter=pcp&month=8&year=1923&filter=p12&state=6&div=0

National Oceanic and Atmospheric Administration. *Monthly & Seasonal Snowfall at Central Park.* Available at: http://www.erh.noaa.gov/okx/climate/records/monthseasonsnowfall.html

Neighborhoods of Norwich, Connecticut. Available at: http://en.wikipedia.org/wiki/Neighborhoods_of_Norwich,_Connecticut

Norwich Bulletin. Norwich, CT.

Norwich Street Directory: Containing A General Directory of the Citizens, Street Guide, Classified Business Directory, Street Directory, New Map, Record of the City Government, Institutions, etc. New Haven, Price & Lee Company, 1922.

Norwich, City of. Office of the City Clerk.

Okrent, Daniel. Last Call: The Rise and Fall of Prohibition. Scribner, 2010.

Polish Center. Christmas: *Wigilia – Christmas Eve.* Available at:

http://www.polishcenter.org/Christmas/WIGILIA-ENG.htm

Rootsweb. English Equivalents of Foreign Given Names. Available at: http://www.rootsweb.ancestry.com/~scoconee/names.html

Schenone, Laura. A Thousand Years Over a Hot Stove: A History of American Women Told Through Food, Recipes, and Remembrances. W.W. Norton & Co., 2003.

Smith, George F., MD, and Dharmapuri Vidyasagar, MD. *Perspectives in Neonatology.* Historical Review and Recent Advances in Neonatal and Perinatal Medicine. Mead Johnson Nutritional Division, 1980. Available at: http://www.neonatology.org/classics/mj1980/default.html

St. Joseph's Catholic Church. Norwich, CT.

St. Nicholas Orthodox Church. Norwich, CT. 95th Anniversary 1915-2010.

Statue of Liberty Ellis Island Foundation, Inc. http://www.ellisisland.org/

Sutherland, John F. *Immigration to Connecticut.* Connecticut's Heritage Gateway. Available at: http://www.ctheritage.org/encyclopedia/topicalsur veys/immigration.htm

Topoquest. USGS Map Name: Norwich, CT. Available at: http://www.topoquest.com/map.php?lat=41.57552 &lon=- 72.11028&datum=nad27&zoom=4&map=auto&coor d=d&mode=zoomin&size=m

Trolley Towns Connecticut. Available at: http://www.bera.org/ttowns.html

U.S. Central Intelligence Agency. The World Factbook. Infant mortality rates are available at: https://www.cia.gov/library/publications/the-world-factbook/rankorder/2091rank.html

U.S. Bureau of the Census. *Birth, Stillbirth, and Infant Mortality Statistics for the Birth Registration Area of the United States.* Annual Report, Part 2. Washington, Government Printing Office, 1929.

U.S. Bureau of the Census. *Live Births, Deaths, Infant Deaths, and Maternal Deaths: 1900-2001.* Statistical Abstract of the United States: 2003. Available at: www.census.gov/statab/hist/HS-13.pdf

U.S. Department of the Interior. National Parks Service. <u>National Register of Historic Places Inventory – Nomination Form</u>. Received October 26, 1982. Available at: pdfhost.focus.nps.gov/docs/NRHP/Text/82001006.pdf

U.S. Heart Lung and Blood Institute. National Institute of Health. *What is Respiratory Distress Syndrome?* Available at: <u>http://www.nhlbi.nih.gov/health/health-topics/topics/rds/</u>

Weathersource.com. <u>Official Weather: 06360</u>.

Wittke, Carl. <u>We Who Built America</u>. Case Western Reserve University, 1967.

Worth, Jennifer. <u>The Midwife: A Memoir of Birth, Joy, and Hard Times</u>. Penguin Group, 2002.

In addition to the sources listed, I used a number of thesauri and English language usage guides, sunrise and sunset information, maps and geographic information, and Polish and Lithuanian pronunciation guides available online for quick reference.

Bernice L. Rocque

CPSIA information can be obtained at www.ICGtesting.com
Printed in the USA
BVOW082156041112

304649BV00001B/3/P